JEEVES TAKES CHARGE

P. G. Wodehouse was born in Guildford, Surrey,
in 1881 and educated at Dulwich College. After
working for the Hong Kong and Shanghai Bank
for two years, he left to earn his living as a
journalist and storywriter.

During his lifetime he wrote over ninety books,
and his work has won worldwide acclaim. He
was hailed by *The Times* as 'A comic genius
recognized in his lifetime as a classic and an old
master of farce.' P. G. Wodehouse said: 'I believe
there are two ways of writing novels. One is mine,
making a sort of musical comedy without music
and ignoring real life altogether; the other is going
right deep down into life and not caring a damn.'

In 1975 he was created a Knight of the British
Empire and he died on St Valentine's Day in the
same year at the age of ninety-three.

P. G. Wodehouse

JEEVES TAKES CHARGE

And Other Stories

ARROW BOOKS

Arrow Books Limited
20 Vauxhall Bridge Road, London SW1V 2SA

An imprint of Random Century Group

London Melbourne Sydney Auckland
Johannesburg and agencies throughout
the world

First published by Arrow 1990

The stories in this collection first appeared in

CARRY ON JEEVES © P. G. Wodehouse 1925, 1927, 1956
Jeeves Takes Charge

THE INIMITABLE JEEVES © P. G. Wodehouse 1973
The Pride of the Woosters is Wounded
The Hero's Reward
Introducing Claude and Eustace
Sir Roderick Comes to Lunch
Comrade Bingo
Bingo has a Bad Goodwood
The Great Sermon Handicap
The Purity of the Turf

VERY GOOD, JEEVES © P. G. Wodehouse 1930
Jeeves and the Yule-tide Spirit
Jeeves and the Song of Songs
Episode of the Dog McIntosh
Indian Summer of an Uncle

Phototypeset by Input Typesetting Ltd, London

Printed and bound in Great Britain by
Courier International Ltd, Tiptree, Essex

ISBN 0 09 977760 6

To Bernard le Strange
and
E. Phillips Oppenheim

CONTENTS

=1=
JEEVES TAKES CHARGE

Now, touching this business of old Jeeves – my man, you know – how do we stand? Lots of people think I'm much too dependent on him. My Aunt Agatha, in fact, has even gone so far as to call him my keeper. Well, what I say is: Why not? The man's a genius. From the collar upward he stands alone. I gave up trying to run my own affairs within a week of his coming to me. That was about half a dozen years ago, directly after the rather rummy business of Florence Craye, my Uncle Willoughby's book, and Edwin, the Boy Scout.

The thing really began when I got back to Easeby, my uncle's place in Shropshire. I was spending a week or so there, as I generally did in the summer; and I had had to break my visit to come back to London to get a new valet. I had found Meadowes, the fellow I had taken to Easeby with me, sneaking my silk socks, a thing no bloke of spirit could stick at any price. It transpiring, moreover, that he had looted a lot of other things here and there about the place. I was reluctantly compelled to hand the misguided blighter the mitten and go to London to ask the registry office to dig up another specimen for my approval. They sent me Jeeves.

I shall always remember the morning he came. It so happened that the night before I had been present at a rather cheery little supper, and I was feeling pretty rocky. On top of this I was trying to read a book Florence Craye had given me. She had been one of the

1

house-party at Easeby, and two or three days before I left we had got engaged. I was due back at the end of the week, and I knew she would expect me to have finished the book by then. You see, she was particularly keen on boosting me up a bit nearer her own plane of intellect. She was a girl with a wonderful profile, but steeped to the gills in serious purpose. I can't give you a better idea of the way things stood than by telling you that the book she'd given me to read was called *Types of Ethical Theory*, and that when I opened it at random I struck a page beginning:

The postulate or common understanding involved in speech is certainly co-extensive, in the obligation it carries, with the social organism of which language is the instrument, and the ends of which it is an effort to subserve.

All perfectly true, no doubt; but not the sort of thing to spring on a lad with a morning head.

I was doing my best to skim through this bright little volume when the bell rang. I crawled off the sofa and opened the door. A kind of darkish sort of respectful Johnnie stood without.

'I was sent by the agency, sir,' he said. 'I was given to understand that you require a valet.'

I'd have preferred an undertaker; but I told him to stagger in, and he floated noiselessly through the doorway like a healing zephyr. That impressed me from the start. Meadowes had had flat feet and used to clump. This fellow didn't seem to have any feet at all. He just streamed in. He had a grave, sympathetic face, as if he, too, knew what it was to sup with the lads.

'Excuse me, sir,' he said gently.

Then he seemed to flicker, and wasn't there any

longer. I heard him moving about in the kitchen, and presently he came back with a glass on a tray.

'If you would drink this, sir,' he said, with a kind of bedside manner, rather like the royal doctor shooting the bracer into the sick prince. 'It is a little preparation of my own invention. It is the Worcester Sauce that gives it colour. The raw egg makes it nutritious. The red pepper gives it its bite. Gentlemen have told me they have found it extremely invigorating after a late evening.'

I would have clutched at anything that looked like a lifeline that morning. I swallowed the stuff. For a moment I felt as if somebody had touched off a bomb inside the old bean and was strolling down my throat with a lighted torch, and then everything seemed suddenly to get all right. The sun shone in through the window; birds twittered in the tree-tops; and, generally speaking, hope dawned once more.

'You're engaged!' I said, as soon as I could say anything.

I perceived clearly that this cove was one of the world's workers, the sort no home should be without.

'Thank you, sir. My name is Jeeves.'

'You can start in at once?'

'Immediately, sir.'

'Because I'm due down at Easeby, in Shropshire, the day after tomorrow.'

'Very good, sir.' He looked past me at the mantelpiece. 'That is an excellent likeness of Lady Florence Craye, sir. It is two years since I saw her ladyship. I was at one time in Lord Worplesdon's employment. I tendered my resignation because I could not see eye to eye with his lordship in his desire to dine in dress trousers, a flannel shirt, and a shooting coat.'

He couldn't tell me anything I didn't know about

the old boy's eccentricity. This Lord Worplesdon was Florence's father. He was the old buster who, a few years later, came down to breakfast one morning, lifted the first cover he saw, said "Eggs! Eggs! Eggs! Damn all eggs!" in an overwrought sort of voice, and instantly legged it for France, never to return to the bosom of his family. This, mind you, being a bit of luck for the bosom of the family, for old Worplesdon had the worst temper in the county.

I had known the family ever since I was a kid, and from boyhood up this old boy had put the fear of death into me. Time, the great healer, could never remove from my memory the occasion when he found me – then a stripling of fifteen – smoking one of his special cigars in the stables. He got after me with a hunting-crop just at the moment when I was beginning to realize that what I wanted most on earth was solitude and repose, and chased me more than a mile across difficult country. If there was a flaw, so to speak, in the pure joy of being engaged to Florence, it was the fact that she rather took after her father, and one was never certain when she might erupt. She had a wonderful profile, though.

'Lady Florence and I are engaged, Jeeves,' I said.

'Indeed, sir?'

You know, there was a kind of rummy something about his manner. Perfectly all right and all that, but not what you'd call chirpy. It somehow gave me the impression that he wasn't keen on Florence. Well, of course, it wasn't my business. I supposed that while he had been valeting old Worplesdon she must have trodden on his toes in some way. Florence was a dear girl, and, seen sideways, most awfully good-looking; but if she had a fault it was a tendency to be a bit imperious with the domestic staff.

4

At this point in the proceedings there was another ring at the front door. Jeeves shimmered out and came back with a telegram. I opened it. It ran:

Return immediately. Extremely urgent. Catch first train. Florence.

'Rum!' I said.
'Sir?'
'Oh, nothing!'
It shows how little I knew Jeeves in those days that I didn't go a bit deeper into the matter with him. Nowadays I would never dream of reading a rummy communication without asking him what he thought of it. And this one was devilish odd. What I mean is, Florence knew I was going back to Easeby the day after tomorrow, anyway; so why the hurry call? Something must have happened, of course; but I couldn't see what on earth it could be.

'Jeeves,' I said, 'we shall be going down to Easeby this afternoon. Can you manage it?'
'Certainly, sir.'
'You can get your packing done and all that?'
'Without any difficulty, sir. Which suit will you wear for the journey?'
'This one.'
I had on a rather sprightly young check that morning, to which I was a good deal attached; I fancied it, in fact, more than a little. It was perhaps rather sudden till you got used to it, but, nevertheless, an extremely sound effort, which many lads at the club and elsewhere had admired unrestrainedly.

'Very good, sir.'
Again there was that kind of rummy something in his manner. It was the way he said it, don't you know. He didn't like the suit. I pulled myself together to assert

myself. Something seemed to tell me that, unless I was jolly careful and nipped this lad in the bud, he would be starting to boss me. He had the aspect of a distinctly resolute blighter.

Well, I wasn't going to have any of that sort of thing, by Jove! I'd seen so many cases of fellows who had become perfect slaves to their valets. I remember poor old Aubrey Fothergill telling me – with absolute tears in his eyes, poor chap! – one night at the club, that he had been compelled to give up a favourite pair of brown shoes simply because Meekyn, his man, disapproved of them. You have to keep these fellows in their place, don't you know. You have to work the good old iron-hand-in-the-velvet-glove wheeze. If you give them a what's-its-name, they take a thingummy.

'Don't you like this suit, Jeeves?' I said coldly.

'Oh, yes, sir.'

'Well, what don't you like about it?'

'It is a very nice suit, sir.'

'Well, what's wrong with it? Out with it, dash it!'

'If I might make the suggestion, sir, a simple brown or blue, with a hint of some quiet twill – '

'What absolute rot!'

'Very good, sir.'

'Perfectly blithering, my dear man!'

'As you say, sir.'

I felt as if I had stepped on the place where the last stair ought to have been, but wasn't. I felt defiant, if you know what I mean, and there didn't seem anything to defy.

'All right, then,' I said.

'Yes, sir.'

And then he went away to collect his kit, while I started in again on *Types of Ethical Theory* and took a stab at a chapter headed "Idiopsychological Ethics".

Most of the way down in the train that afternoon, I was wondering what could be up at the other end. I simply couldn't see what could have happened. Easeby wasn't one of those country houses you read about in the society novels, where young girls are lured on to play baccarat and then skinned to the bone of their jewellery, and so on. The house-party I had left had consisted entirely of law-abiding birds like myself.

Besides, my uncle wouldn't have let anything of that kind go on in his house. He was a rather stiff, precise sort of old boy, who liked a quiet life. He was just finishing a history of the family or something, which he had been working on for the last year, and didn't stir much from the library. He was rather a good instance of what they say about its being a good scheme for a fellow to sow his wild oats. I'd been told that in his youth Uncle Willoughby had been a bit of a bounder. You would never have thought it to look at him now.

When I got to the house, Oakshott, the butler, told me that Florence was in her room, watching her maid pack. Apparently there was a dance on at a house about twenty miles away that night, and she was motoring over with some of the Easeby lot and would be away some nights. Oakshott said she had told him to tell her the moment I arrived; so I trickled into the smoking-room and waited, and presently in she came. A glance showed me that she was perturbed, and even peeved. Her eyes had a goggly look, and altogether she appeared considerably pipped.

'Darling!' I said, and attempted the good old embrace; but she side-stepped like a bantam-weight.

'Don't!'

'What's the matter?'

'Everything's the matter! Bertie, you remember asking

7

me, when you left, to make myself pleasant to your uncle?'

'Yes.'

The idea being, of course, that as at the time I was more or less dependent on Uncle Willoughby I couldn't very well marry without his approval. And though I knew he wouldn't have any objection to Florence, having known her father since they were at Oxford together, I hadn't wanted to take any chances; so I had told her to make an effort to fascinate the old boy.

'You told me it would please him particularly if I asked him to read me some of his history of the family.'

'Wasn't he pleased.'

'He was delighted. He finished writing the thing yesterday afternoon, and read me nearly all of it last night. I have never had such a shock in my life. The book is an outrage. It is impossible. It is horrible!'

'But, dash it, the family weren't so bad as all that.'

'It is not a history of the family at all. Your uncle has written his reminiscences! He calls them *Recollections of a Long Life!*'

I began to understand. As I say, Uncle Willoughby had been somewhat on the tabasco side as a young man, and it began to look as if he might have turned out something pretty fruity if he had started recollecting his long life.

'If half of what he has written is true,' said Florence, 'your uncle's youth must have been perfectly appalling. The moment we began to read he plunged straight into a most scandalous story of how he and my father were thrown out of a music-hall in 1887!'

'Why?'

'I decline to tell you why.'

It must have been something pretty bad. It took a lot to make them chuck people out of music-halls in 1887.

'Your uncle specifically states that father had drunk a quart and a half of champagne before beginning the evening,' she went on. 'The book is full of stories like that. There is a dreadful one about Lord Emsworth.'

'Lord Emsworth? Not the one we know? Not the one at Blandings?'

A most respectable old Johnnie, don't you know. Doesn't do a thing nowadays but dig in the garden with a spud.

'The very same. That is what makes the book so unspeakable. It is full of stories about people one knows who are the essence of propriety today, but who seem to have behaved, when they were in London in the eighties, in a manner that would not have been tolerated in the fo'c'sle of a whaler. Your uncle seems to remember everything disgraceful that happened to anybody when he was in his early twenties. There is a story about Sir Stanley Gervase-Gervase at Rosherville Gardens which is ghastly in its perfection of detail. It seems that Sir Stanley — but I can't tell you!'

'Have a dash!'

'No!'

'Oh, well, I shouldn't worry. No publisher will print the book if it's as bad as all that.'

'On the contrary, your uncle told me that all negotiations are settled with Riggs and Ballinger, and he's sending off the manuscript tomorrow for immediate publication. They make a special thing of that sort of book. They published Lady Carnaby's *Memories of Eighty Interesting Years*.'

'I read 'em!'

'Well, then, when I tell you that Lady Carnaby's *Memories* are simply not to be compared with your uncle's *Recollections*, you will understand my state of mind. And father appears in nearly every story in the

book! I am horrified at the things he did when he was
a young man!'

'What's to be done?'

'The manuscript must be intercepted before it reaches
Riggs and Ballinger, and destroyed!'

I sat up.

This sounded rather sporting.

'How are you going to do it?' I inquired.

'How can I do it? Didn't I tell you the parcel goes
off tomorrow? I am going to the Murgatroyds' dance
tonight and shall not be back till Monday. You must
do it. That is why I telegraphed to you.'

'What!'

She gave me a look.

'Do you mean to say you refuse to help me, Bertie?'

'No; but – I say!'

'It's quite simple.'

'But even if I – What I mean is – Of course, anything
I can do – but – if you know what I mean – '

'You say you want to marry me, Bertie?'

'Yes, of course; but still – '

For a moment she looked exactly like her old father.

'I will never marry you if those *Recollections* are
published.'

'But, Florence, old thing!'

'I mean it. You may look on it as a test, Bertie. If
you have the resource and courage to carry this thing
through, I will take it as evidence that you are not the
vapid and shiftless person most people think you. If you
fail, I shall know that your Aunt Agatha was right when
she called you a spineless invertebrate and advised me
strongly not to marry you. It will be perfectly simple
for you to intercept the manuscript, Bertie. It only
requires a little resolution.'

'But suppose Uncle Willoughby catches me at it? He'd cut me off with a bob.'

'If you care more for your uncle's money than for me – '

'No, no! Rather not!'

'Very well, then. The parcel containing the manuscript will, of course, be placed on the hall table tomorrow for Oakshott to take to the village with the letters. All you have to do is to take it away and destroy it. Then your uncle will think it has been lost in the post.'

It sounded thin to me.

'Hasn't he got a copy of it?'

'No; it has not been typed. He is sending the manuscript just as he wrote it.'

'But he could write it over again.'

'As if he would have the energy!'

'But – '

'If you are going to do nothing but make absurd objections, Bertie – '

'I was only pointing things out.'

'Well, don't! Once and for all, will you do me this quite simple act of kindness?'

The way she put it gave me an idea.

'Why not get Edwin to do it? Keep it in the family, kind of, don't you know. Besides, it would be a boon to the kid.'

A jolly bright idea it seemed to me. Edwin was her young brother, who was spending his holidays at Easeby. He was a ferret-faced kid, whom I had disliked since birth. As a matter of fact, talking of Recollections and Memories, it was young blighted Edwin who, nine years before, had led his father to where I was smoking his cigar and caused all the unpleasantness. He was fourteen now and had just joined the Boy Scouts. He was one of those thorough kids, and took his responsibilities pretty seriously. He was always in a sort of fever because he was dropping behind schedule with his daily acts of kindness. However hard he tried, he'd fall behind; and then you would find him prowling about the house, setting such a clip to try and catch up with himself that Easeby was rapidly becoming a perfect hell for man and beast.

The idea didn't seem to strike Florence.

'I shall do nothing of the kind, Bertie. I wonder you can't appreciate the compliment I am paying you – trusting you like this.'

'Oh, I see that all right, but what I mean is, Edwin would do it so much better than I would. These Boy Scouts are up to all sorts of dodges. They spoor, don't you know, and take cover and creep about, and what not.'

'Bertie, will you or will you not do this perfectly trivial thing for me? If not, say so now, and let us end this farce of pretending that you care a snap of the fingers for me.'

'Dear old soul, I love you devotedly!'

'Then will you or will you not – '

'Oh, all right,' I said. 'All right! All right! All right!'

And then I tottered forth to think it over. I met Jeeves in the passage just outside.

'I beg your pardon, sir. I was endeavouring to find you.'

'What's the matter?'

'I felt that I should tell you, sir, that somebody has been putting black polish on our brown walking shoes.'

'What! Who? Why?'

'I could not say, sir.'

'Can anything be done with them?'

'Nothing, sir.'

'Damn!'

'Very good, sir.'

I've wondered since then how these murderer fellows manage to keep in shape while they're contemplating their next effort. I had a much simpler sort of job on hand, and the thought of it rattled me to such an extent in the night watches that I was a perfect wreck next day. Dark circles under the eyes – I give you my word! I had to call on Jeeves to rally round with one of those lifesavers of his.

From breakfast on I felt like a bag-snatcher at a railway station. I had to hang about waiting for the parcel to be put on the hall table, and it wasn't put. Uncle Willoughby was a fixture in the library, adding the finishing touches to the great work, I supposed, and the more I thought the thing over the less I liked it. The chances against my pulling it off seemed about three to two, and the thought of what would happen if I didn't gave me cold shivers down the spine. Uncle Willoughby was a pretty mild sort of old boy, as a rule, but I've known him to cut up rough, and, by Jove, he was scheduled to extend himself if he caught me trying to get away with his life work.

It wasn't till nearly four that he toddled out of the library with the parcel under his arm, put it on the table, and toddled off again. I was hiding a bit to the south-east at the moment, behind a suit of armour. I bounded out and legged it for the table. Then I nipped upstairs to hide the swag. I charged in like a mustang and nearly stubbed my toe on young blighted Edwin, the Boy Scout. He was standing at the chest of drawers, confound him, messing about with my ties.

'Hallo!' he said.

'What are you doing here?'

'I'm tidying your room. It's my last Saturday's act of kindness.'

'Last Saturday's.'

'I'm five days behind. I was six till last night, but I polished your shoes.'

'Was it you – '

'Yes. Did you see them? I just happened to think of it. I was in here, looking round. Mr Berkeley had this room while you were away. He left this morning. I thought perhaps he might have left something in it that I could have sent on. I've often done acts of kindness that way.'

'You must be a comfort to one and all!'

It became more and more apparent to me that this infernal kid must somehow be turned out eftsoons or right speedily. I had hidden the parcel behind my back, and I didn't think he had seen it; but I wanted to get at that chest of drawers quick, before anyone else came along.

'I shouldn't bother about tidying the room,' I said.

'I like tidying it. It's not a bit of trouble – really.'

'But it's quite tidy now.'

'Not so tidy as I shall make it.'

This was getting perfectly rotten. I didn't want to murder the kid, and yet there didn't seem any other way of shifting him. I pressed down the mental accelerator. The old lemon throbbed fiercely. I got an idea.

'There's something much kinder than that which you could do,' I said. 'You see that box of cigars? Take it down to the smoking-room and snip off the ends for me. That would save me no end of trouble. Stagger along, laddie.'

He seemed a bit doubtful; but he staggered. I shoved the parcel into a drawer, locked it, trousered the key, and felt better. I might be a chump, but, dash it, I could

14

out-general a mere kid with a face like a ferret. I went downstairs again. Just as I was passing the smoking-room door out curveted Edwin. It seemed to me that if he wanted to do a real act of kindness he would commit suicide.

'I'm snipping them,' he said.

'Snip on! Snip on!'

'Do you like them snipped much, or only a bit?'

'Medium.'

'All right. I'll be getting on, then'.

'I should.'

And we parted.

Fellows who know all about that sort of thing – detectives, and so on – will tell you that the most difficult thing in the world is to get rid of the body. I remember, as a kid, having to learn by heart a poem about a bird by the name of Eugene Aram, who had the deuce of a job in this respect. All I can recall of the actual poetry is the bit that goes:

> Tum-tum, tum-tum, tum-tumty-tum,
> I slew him, tum-tum tum!

But I recollect that the poor blighter spent much of his valuable time dumping the corpse into ponds and burying it, and what not, only to have it pop out at him again. It was about an hour after I had shoved the parcel into the drawer when I realized that I had let myself in for just the same sort of thing.

Florence had talked in an airy sot of way about destroying the manuscript; but when one came down to it, how the deuce can a chap destroy a great chunky mass of paper in somebody else's house in the middle of summer? I couldn't ask to have a fire in my bedroom, with the thermometer in the eighties. And if I didn't burn the thing, how else could I get rid of it? Fellows on the battlefield eat dispatches to keep them from falling into the hands of the enemy, but it would have taken me a year to eat Uncle Willoughby's *Recollections.*

I'm bound to say the problem absolutely baffled me. The only thing seemed to be to leave the parcel in the drawer and hope for the best.

I don't know whether you have ever experienced it, but it's a dashed unpleasant thing having a crime on one's conscience. Towards the end of the day the mere sight of the drawer began to depress me. I found myself getting all on edge; and once when Uncle Willoughby trickled silently into the smoking-room when I was alone there and spoke to me before I knew he was there, I broke the record for the sitting high jump.

I was wondering all the time when Uncle Willoughby would sit up and take notice. I didn't think he would have time to suspect that anything had gone wrong till Saturday morning, when he would be expecting, of course, to get the acknowledgement of the manuscript from the publishers. But early on Friday evening he came out of the library as I was passing and asked me to step in. He was looking considerably rattled.

'Bertie,' he said – he always spoke in a precise sort of pompous kind of way – 'an exceedingly disturbing thing has happened. As you know, I dispatched the manuscript of my book to Messrs Riggs and Ballinger, the publishers, yesterday afternoon. It should have reached them by the first post this morning. Why I should have been uneasy I cannot say, but my mind was not altogether at rest respecting the safety of the parcel. I therefore telephoned to Messrs Riggs and Ballinger a few moments back to make inquiries. To my consternation they informed me that they were not yet in receipt of my manuscript.'

'Very rum!'

'I recollect distinctly placing it myself on the hall table in good time to be taken to the village. But here is a sinister thing. I have spoken to Oakshott, who took the rest of the letters to the post office, and he cannot recall seeing it there. He is, indeed, unswerving in his assertions that when he went to the hall to collect the letters there was no parcel among them.'

'Sounds funny!'

'Bertie, shall I tell you what I suspect?'

'What's that?'

'The suspicion will no doubt sound to you incredible, but it alone seems to fit the facts as we know them. I incline to the belief that the parcel has been stolen.'

'Oh, I say! Surely not!'

'Wait! Hear me out. Though I have said nothing to you before, or to anyone else, concerning the matter, the fact remains that during the past few weeks a number of objects – some valuable, others not – have disappeared in this house. The conclusion to which one is irresistibly impelled is that we have a kleptomaniac in our midst. It is a peculiarity of kleptomania, as you are no doubt aware, that the subject is unable to differentiate between the intrinsic values of objects. He will purloin an old coat as readily as a diamond ring, or a tobacco pipe costing but a few shillings with the same eagerness as a purse of gold. The fact that this manuscript of mine could be of no possible value to any outside person convinces me that – '

'But, uncle, one moment; I know all about those things that were stolen. It was Meadowes, my man, who pinched them. I caught him snaffling my silk socks. Right in the act, by Jove!'

He was tremendously impressed.

'You amaze me, Bertie! Send for the man at once and question him.'

'But he isn't here. You see, directly I found that he was a sock-sneaker I gave him the boot. That's why I went to London – to get a new man.'

'Then, if the man Meadowes is no longer in the house it could not be he who purloined my manuscript. The whole thing is inexplicable.'

After which we brooded for a bit. Uncle Willoughby pottered about the room, registering baf
fledness, while I sat sucking at a cigarette, feeling rather like a chappie I'd once read about in a book, who murdered another cove and hid the body under the dining-room table, and then had to be the life and soul of a dinner party, with it there all the time. My guilty secret oppressed me to such an extent that after a while I couldn't stick it any longer. I lit another cigarette and started for a stroll in the grounds, by way of cooling off.

It was one of those still evenings you get in the summer, when you can hear a snail clear its throat a mile away. The sun was sinking over the hills and the gnats were fooling about all over the place, and every-thing smelled rather topping – what with the falling dew and so on – and I was just beginning to feel a little soothed by the peace of it all when suddenly I heard my name spoken.

'It's about Bertie.'

It was the loathsome voice of young blighted Edwin! For a moment I couldn't locate it. Then I realized that it came from the library. My stroll had taken me within a few yards of the open window.

I had often wondered how those Johnnies in books did it – I mean the fellows with whom it was the work of a moment to do about a dozen things that ought to have taken them about ten minutes. But, as a matter of fact, it was the work of a moment with me to chuck away my cigarette, swear a bit, leap about ten yards, dive into a bush that stood near the library window, and stand there with my ears flapping. I was as certain as I've ever been of anything that all sorts of rotten things were in the offing.

'About Bertie?' I heard Uncle Willoughby say.

'About Bertie and your parcel. I heard you talking to him just now. I believe he's got it.'

When I tell you that just as I heard these frightful words a fairly substantial beetle of sorts dropped from the bush down the back of my neck, and I couldn't even stir to squash the same, you will understand that I felt pretty rotten. Everything seemed against me.

'What do you mean, boy? I was discussing the disappearance of my manuscript with Bertie only a moment back, and he professed himself as perplexed by the mystery as myself.'

'Well, I was in his room yesterday afternoon, doing him an act of kindness, and he came in with a parcel. I could see it, though he tried to keep it behind his back. And then he asked me to go to the smoking-room and snip some cigars for him; and about two minutes afterwards he came down – and he wasn't carrying anything. So it must be in his room.'

I understand they deliberately teach these dashed Boy Scouts to cultivate their powers of observation and education and what not. Devilish thoughtless and inconsiderate of them, I call it. Look at the trouble it causes.

'It sounds incredible,' said Uncle Willoughby, thereby bucking me up a trifle.

'Shall I go and look in his room?' asked young blighted Edwin. 'I'm sure the parcel's there.'

'But what could be his motive for perpetrating this extraordinary theft?'

'Perhaps he's a – what you said just now.'

'A kleptomaniac! Impossible!'

'It might have been Bertie who took all those things from the very start,' suggested the little brute hopefully. 'He may be like Raffles.'

'Raffles?'

'He's a chap in a book who went about pinching things.'

'I cannot believe that Bertie would – ah – go about pinching things.'

'Well, I'm sure he's got the parcel. I'll tell you what you might do. You might say that Mr Berkeley wired that he had left something here. He had Bertie's room, you know. You might say you wanted to look for it.'

'That would be possible. I – '

I didn't wait to hear any more. Things were getting too hot. I sneaked softly out of my bush and raced for the front door. I sprinted up to my room and made for the drawer where I had put the parcel. And then I found I hadn't the key. It wasn't for the deuce of a time that I recollected I had shifted it to my evening trousers the night before and must have forgotten to take it out again.

Where the dickens were my evening things? I had looked all over the place before I remembered that Jeeves must have taken them away to brush. To leap at the bell and ring it was, with me, the work of a moment. I had just rung it when there was a footstep outside, and in came Uncle Willoughby.

'Oh, Bertie,' he said, without a blush, 'I have – ah – received a telegram from Berkeley, who occupied this room in your absence, asking me to forward him his – er – his cigarette-case, which, it would appear, he inadvertently omitted to take with him when he left the house. I cannot find it downstairs; and it has, therefore, occurred to me that he may have left it in this room. I will – er – just take a look round.'

It was one of the most disgusting spectacles I've ever seen – this white-haired old man, who should have been thinking of the hereafter, standing there lying like an actor.

'I haven't seen it anywhere,' I said.

'Nevertheless, I will search. I must – ah – spare no effort.'

'I should have seen it if it had been here – what?'

'It may have escaped your notice. It is – er – possibly in one of the drawers.'

He began to nose about. He pulled out drawer after drawer, pottering round like an old bloodhound, and babbling from time to time about Berkeley and his cigarette-case in a way that struck me as perfectly ghastly. I just stood there, losing weight every moment.

Then he came to the drawer where the parcel was.

'This appears to be locked,' he said, rattling the handle.

'Yes; I shouldn't bother about that one. It – it's – er – locked, and all that sort of thing.'

'You have not the key?'

A soft, respectable voice spoke behind me.

'I fancy, sir, that this must be the key you require. It was in the pocket of your evening trousers.'

It was Jeeves. He had shimmered in, carrying my evening things, and was standing there holding out the key. I could have massacred the man.

'Thank you,' said my uncle.

'Not at all, sir.'

The next moment Uncle Willoughby had opened the drawer. I shut my eyes.

'No,' said Uncle Willoughby, 'there is nothing here. The drawer is empty. Thank you, Bertie. I hope I have not disturbed you. I fancy – er – Berkeley must have taken his case with him after all.'

When he had gone I shut the door carefully. Then I turned to Jeeves. The man was putting my evening things out on a chair.

'Er – Jeeves!'

'Sir?'

'Oh, nothing.'

It was deuced difficult to know how to begin.

'Er – Jeeves!'

'Sir?'

'Did you – Was there – Have you by chance–'

'I removed the parcel this morning, sir.'

'Oh – ah – why?'

'I considered it more prudent, sir.'

I mused for a while.

'Of course, I suppose all this seems tolerably rummy to you, Jeeves?'

'Not at all, sir. I chanced to overhear you and Lady Florence speaking of the matter the other evening, sir.'

'Did you, by Jove?'

'Yes, sir.'

'Well – er – Jeeves, I think that, on the whole, if you were to – as it were – freeze on to that parcel until we get back to London–'

'Exactly, sir.'

'And then we might – er – so to speak – chuck it away somewhere – what?'

'Precisely, sir.'

'I'll leave it in your hands.'

'Entirely, sir.'

'You know, Jeeves, you're by way of being rather a topper.'

'I endeavour to give satisfaction, sir.'
'One in a million, by Jove!'
'It is very kind of you to say so, sir.'
'Well, that's about all, then, I think.'
'Very good, sir.'

Florence came back on Monday. I didn't see her till we were all having tea in the hall. It wasn't till the crowd had cleared away a bit that we got a chance of having a word together.

'Well, Bertie?' she said.

'It's all right.'

'You have destroyed the manuscript?'

'Not exactly; but – '

'What do you mean?'

'I mean I haven't absolutely – '

'Bertie, your manner is furtive!'

'It's all right. It's this way – '

And I was just going to explain how things stood when out of the library came leaping Uncle Willoughby, looking as braced as a two-year-old. The old boy was a changed man.

'A most remarkable thing, Bertie! I have just been speaking with Mr Riggs on the telephone, and he tells me he received my manuscript by the first post this morning. I cannot imagine what can have caused the delay. Our postal facilities are extremely inadequate in the rural districts. I shall write to headquarters about it. It is insufferable if valuable parcels are to be delayed in this fashion.'

I happened to be looking at Florence's profile at the moment, and at this juncture she swung round and gave me a look that went right through me like a knife. Uncle Willoughby meandered back to the library, and there was a silence that you could have dug bits out of with a spoon.

'I can't understand it,' I said at last. 'I can't understand it, by Jove!'

'I can. I can understand it perfectly, Bertie. Your heart failed you. Rather than risk offending your uncle you – '

'No, no! Absolutely!'

'You preferred to lose me rather than risk losing the money. Perhaps you did not think I meant what I said. I meant every word. Our engagement is ended.'

'But – I say!'

'Not another word!'

'But, Florence, old thing!'

'I do not wish to hear any more. I see now that your Aunt Agatha was perfectly right. I consider that I have had a very lucky escape. There was a time when I thought that, with patience, you might be moulded into something worth while. I see now that you are impossible!'

And she popped off, leaving me to pick up the pieces. When I had collected the debris to some extent I went to my room and rang for Jeeves. He came in looking as if nothing had happened or was ever going to happen. He was the calmest thing in captivity.

'Jeeves!' I yelled. 'Jeeves, that parcel has arrived in London!'

'Yes, sir?'

'Did you send it?'

'Yes, sir. I acted for the best, sir. I think that both you and Lady Florence overestimated the danger of people being offended at being mentioned in Sir Willoughby's *Recollections*. It has been my experience, sir, that the normal person enjoys seeing his or her name in print, irrespective of what is said about them. I have an aunt, sir, who a few years ago was a martyr to swollen limbs. She tried Walkinshaw's Supreme Ointment and obtained considerable relief – so much so that she sent them an unsolicited testimonial. Her pride at seeing her photograph in the daily papers in connexion with descriptions of her lower limbs before taking, which were nothing less than revolting, was so intense that it led me to believe that publicity, of whatever sort, is what nearly everybody desires. Moreover, if you have ever studied psychology, sir, you will know that respectable old gentlemen are by no means averse to having it advertised that they were extremely wild in their youth. I have an uncle–'

I cursed his aunts and his uncles and him and all the rest of the family.

'Do you know that Lady Florence has broken off her engagement with me?'

'Indeed, sir?'

Not a bit of sympathy! I might have been telling him it was a fine day.

'You're sacked!'

'Very good, sir.'

He coughed gently.

'As I am no longer in your employment, sir, I can speak freely without appearing to take a liberty. In my opinion you and Lady Florence were quite unsuitably matched. Her ladyship is of a highly determined and arbitrary temperament, quite opposed to your own. I was in Lord Worplesdon's service for nearly a year, during which time I had ample opportunities of studying her ladyship. The opinion of the servants' hall was far from favourable to her. Her ladyship's temper caused a good deal of adverse comment among us. It was at times quite impossible. You would not have been happy, sir!'

'Get out!'

'I think you would also have found her educational methods a little trying, sir. I have glanced at the book her ladyship gave you – it has been lying on your table since our arrival – and it is, in my opinion, quite unsuitable. You would not have enjoyed it. And I have it from her ladyship's own maid, who happened to overhear a conversation between her ladyship and one of the gentlemen staying here – Mr Maxwell, who is employed in an editorial capacity by one of the reviews – that it was her intention to start you almost immediately upon Nietzsche. You would not enjoy Nietzsche, sir. He is fundamentally unsound.'

'Get out!'

'Very good, sir.'

It's rummy how sleeping on a thing often makes you feel quite different about it. It's happened to me over and over again. Somehow or other, when I woke next morning the old heart didn't feel half so broken as it had done. It was a perfectly topping day, and there was something about the way the sun came in at the window and the row the birds were kicking up in the ivy that made me half wonder whether Jeeves wasn't right. After all, though she had a wonderful profile, was it such a catch being engaged to Florence Craye as the casual observer might imagine? Wasn't there something in what Jeeves had said about her character? I began to realize that my ideal wife was something quite different, something a lot more clinging and drooping and prattling, and what not.

I had got as far as this in thinking the thing out when that *Types of Ethical Theory* caught my eye. I opened it, and I give you my honest word this was what hit me:

Of the two antithetic terms in the Greek philosophy one only was real and self-subsisting; and that one was Ideal Thought as opposed to that which it has to penetrate and mould. The other, corresponding to our Nature, was in itself phenomenal, unreal, without any permanent footing, having no predicates that held true for two moments together; in short, redeemed from negation only by including indwelling realities appearing through.

Well – I mean to say – what? And Nietzsche, from all accounts, a lot worse than that!

'Jeeves,' I said, when he came in with my morning tea, 'I've been thinking it over. You're engaged again.'

'Thank you, sir.'

I sucked down a cheerful mouthful. A great respect for this bloke's judgement began to soak through me.

'Oh, Jeeves,' I said: 'about that check suit.'

'Yes, sir?'

'Is it really a frost?'

'A trifle too bizarre, sir, in my opinion.'

'But lots of fellows have asked me who my tailor is.'

'Doubtless in order to avoid him, sir.'

'He's supposed to be one of the best men in London.'

'I am saying nothing against his moral character, sir.'

I hesitated a bit. I had a feeling that I was passing into this chappie's clutches, and that if I gave in now I should become just like poor old Aubrey Fothergill, unable to call my soul my own. On the other hand, this was obviously a cove of rare intelligence, and it would be a comfort in a lot of ways to have him doing the thinking for me. I made up my mind.

'All right, Jeeves,' I said. 'You know! Give the bally thing away to somebody!'

He looked down at me like a father gazing tenderly at the wayward child.

'Thank you, sir. I gave it to the under-gardener last night. A little more tea, sir?'

=2=
THE PRIDE OF THE
WOOSTERS IS WOUNDED

If there's one thing I like, it's a quiet life. I'm not one of those fellows who get all restless and depressed if things aren't happening to them all the time. You can't make it too placid for me. Give me regular meals, a good show with decent music every now and then, and one or two pals to totter round with, and I ask no more.

That is why the jar, when it came, was such a particularly nasty jar. I mean, I'd returned from Roville with a sort of feeling that from now on, nothing could occur to upset me. Aunt Agatha, I imagined, would require at least a year to recover from the Hemmingway affair; and apart from Aunt Agatha there isn't anybody who really does much in the way of harrying me. It seemed to me that the skies were blue, so to speak, and no clouds in sight.

I little thought . . . Well, look here, what happened was this, and I ask you if it wasn't enough to rattle anybody.

Once a year Jeeves takes a couple of weeks' vacation and biffs off to the sea or somewhere to restore his tissues. Pretty rotten for me, of course, while he's away. But it has to be stuck, so I stick it; and I must admit that he usually manages to get hold of a fairly decent fellow to look after me in his absence.

Well, the time had come round again, and Jeeves was in the kitchen giving the understudy a few tips about his duties. I happened to want a stamp or something, and I toddled down the passage to ask him for it. The silly ass had left the kitchen door open, and I hadn't gone two steps when his voice caught me squarely in the eardrum.

'You will find Mr Wooster,' he was saying to the substitute chappie, 'an exceedingly pleasant and amiable young gentleman, but not intelligent. By no means intelligent. Mentally he is negligible – quite negligible!'

Well, I mean to say, what!

I suppose, strictly speaking, I ought to have charged in and ticked the blighter off properly in no uncertain voice. But I doubt whether it's humanly possible to tick Jeeves off. Personally, I didn't even have a dash at it. I merely called for my hat and stick in a marked manner and legged it. But the memory rankled, if you know what I mean. We Woosters do not lightly forget. At least, we do – some things – appointments, and people's birthdays, and letters to post, and all that – but not an absolute bally insult like the above. I brooded like the dickens.

I was still brooding when I dropped in at the oyster-bar at Buck's for a quick bracer. I needed a bracer rather particularly at the moment, because I was on my way to lunch with Aunt Agatha. A pretty frightful ordeal, believe me or believe me not, even though I took it that after what had happened at Roville she would be in a fairly subdued and amiable mood. I had just had one quick and another rather slower, and was feeling about as cheerio as was possible under the circs, when a muffled voice hailed me from the north-east, and, turning round, I saw young Bingo Little propped up in a corner, wrapping himself round a sizeable chunk of bread and cheese.

'Hallo-allo-allo!' I said. 'Haven't seen you for ages. You've not been in here lately, have you?'

'No. I've been living out in the country.'

'Eh?' I said, for Bingo's loathing for the country was well known. 'Whereabouts?'

'Down in Hampshire, at a place called Ditteredge.'

'No, really? I know some people who've got a house there. The Glossops. Have you met them?'

'Why, that's where I'm staying!' said young Bingo. 'I'm tutoring the Glossop kid.'

'What for?' I said. I couldn't seem to see young Bingo as a tutor. Though, of course, he did get a degree of sorts at Oxford, and I suppose you can always fool some of the people some of the time.

'What for? For money, of course! An absolute sitter came unstitched in the second race at Haydock Park,' said young Bingo, with some bitterness, 'and I dropped my entire month's allowance. I hadn't the nerve to touch my uncle for any more, so it was a case of buzzing round to the agents and getting a job. I've been down there three weeks.'

'I haven't met the Glossop kid.'

'Don't!' advised Bingo, briefly.

'The only one of the family I really know is the girl.' I had hardly spoken these words when the most extraordinary change came over young Bingo's face. His eyes bulged, his cheeks flushed, and his Adam's apple hopped about like one of those india-rubber balls on the top of the fountain in a shooting-gallery.

'Oh, Bertie!' he said, in a strangled sort of voice.

I looked at the poor fish anxiously. I knew that he was always falling in love with someone, but it didn't seem possible that even he could have fallen in love

31

with Honoria Glossop. To me the girl was simply nothing more nor less than a pot of poison. One of those dashed large, brainy, strenuous, dynamic girls you see so many of these days. She had been at Girton, where, in addition to enlarging her brain to the most frightful extent, she had gone in for every kind of sport and developed the physique of a middle-weight catch-as-catch-can wrestler. I'm not sure she didn't box for the Varsity while she was up. The effect she had on me whenever she appeared was to make me want to slide into a cellar and lie low till they blew the All-Clear.

Yet here was young Bingo obviously all for her. There was no mistaking it. The love-light was in the blighter's eyes.

'I worship her, Bertie! I worship the very ground she treads on!' continued the patient, in a loud, penetrating voice. Fred Thompson and one or two fellows had come in, and McGarry, the chappie behind the bar, was listening with his ears flapping. But there's no reticence about Bingo. He always reminds me of the hero of a musical comedy who takes the centre of the stage, gathers the boys round him in a circle, and tells them all about his love at the top of his voice.

'Have you told her?'

'No. I haven't the nerve. But we walk together in the garden most evenings, and it sometimes seems to me that there is a look in her eyes.'

'I know that look. Like a sergeant-major.'

'Nothing of the kind! Like a tender goddess.'

'Half a second, old thing,' I said. 'Are you sure we're talking about the same girl? The one I mean is Honoria. Perhaps there's a younger sister or something I've not heard of?'

'Her name is Honoria,' bawled Bingo reverently.

'And she strikes you as a tender goddess?'

'She does.'

'God bless you!' I said.

'She walks in beauty like the night of cloudless climes and starry skies; and all that's best of dark and bright meet in her aspect and her eyes. Another bit of bread and cheese,' he said to the lad behind the bar.

'You're keeping your strength up,' I said.

'This is my lunch. I've got to meet Oswald at Waterloo at one-fifteen, to catch the train back. I brought him up to town to see the dentist.'

'Oswald? Is that the kid?'

'Yes. Pestilential to a degree.'

'Pestilential! That reminds me, I'm lunching with my Aunt Agatha. I'll have to pop off now, or I'll be late.'

I hadn't seen Aunt Agatha since that little affair of the pearls; and, while I didn't anticipate any great pleasure from gnawing a bone in her society, I must say that there was one topic of conversation I felt pretty confident she wouldn't touch on, and that was the subject of my matrimonial future. I mean, when a woman's made a bloomer like the one Aunt Agatha made at Roville, you'd naturally think that a decent shame would keep her off it for, at any rate, a month or two.

But women beat me. I mean to say, as regards nerve. You'll hardly credit it, but she actually started in on me with the fish. Absolutely with the fish, I give you my solemn word. We'd hardly exchanged a word about the weather, when she let me have it without a blush.

'Bertie,' she said. 'I've been thinking again about you and how necessary it is that you should get married. I quite admit that I was dreadfully mistaken in my opinion of that terrible, hypocritical girl at Roville, but this time there is no danger of an error. By great good luck I have found the very wife for you, a girl whom I have only recently met, but whose family is above

33

suspicion. She has plenty of money, too, though that does not matter in your case. The great point is that she is strong, self-reliant and sensible, and will counter-balance the deficiencies and weaknesses of your character. She has met you; and, while there is naturally much in you of which she disapproves, she does not dislike you. I know this, for I have sounded her – guardedly, of course – and I am sure that you have only to make the first advances – '

'Who is it?' I would have said it long before, but the shock had made me swallow a bit of roll the wrong way, and I had only just finished turning purple and trying to get a bit of air back into the old windpipe. 'Who is it?'

'Sir Roderick Glossop's daughter, Honoria.'

'No, no!' I cried, paling beneath the tan.

'Don't be silly, Bertie. She is just the wife for you.'

'Yes, but look here – '

'She will mould you.'

'But I don't want to be moulded.'

Aunt Agatha gave me the kind of look she used to give me when I was a kid and had been found in the jam cupboard.

'Bertie! I hope you are not going to be troublesome.'

'Well, but I mean – '

'Lady Glossop has very kindly invited you to Ditteredge Hall for a few days. I told her you would be delighted to come down tomorrow.'

'I'm sorry, but I've got a dashed important engagement tomorrow.'

'What engagement?'

'Well – er – '

'You have no engagement. And, even if you had, you must put it off. I shall be very seriously annoyed, Bertie, if you do not go to Ditteredge Hall tomorrow.'

'Oh, right-o!' I said.

It wasn't two minutes after I had parted from Aunt Agatha before the old fighting spirit of the Woosters reasserted itself. Ghastly as the peril was which loomed before me, I was conscious of a rummy sort of exhilaration. It was a tight corner, but the tighter the corner, I felt, the more juicily should I score off Jeeves when I got myself out of it without a bit of help from him. Ordinarily, of course, I should have consulted him and trusted to him to solve the difficulty; but after what I had heard him saying in the kitchen, I was dashed if I was going to demean myself. When I got home I addressed the man with light abandon.

'Jeeves,' I said, 'I'm in a bit of a difficulty.'

'I'm sorry to hear that, sir.'

'Yes, quite a bad hole. In fact, you might say on the brink of a precipice, and faced by an awful doom.'

'If I could be of any assistance, sir – '

'Oh, no. No, no. Thanks very much, but no, no. I won't trouble you. I've no doubt I shall be able to get out of it by myself.'

'Very good, sir.'

So that was that. I'm bound to say I'd have welcomed a bit more curiosity from the fellow, but that is Jeeves all over. Cloaks his emotions, if you know what I mean.

Honoria was away when I got to Ditteredge on the following afternoon. Her mother told me that she was staying with some people named Braythwayt in the neighbourhood, and would be back next day, bringing the daughter of the house with her for a visit. She said I would find Oswald out in the grounds, and such is a mother's love that she spoke as if that were a bit of a boost for the grounds and an inducement to go there.

Rather decent, the grounds at Ditteredge. A couple of terraces, a bit of lawn with a cedar on it, a bit of shrubbery, and finally a small but goodish lake with a stone bridge running across it. Directly I'd worked my way round the shrubbery I spotted young Bingo leaning against the bridge smoking a cigarette. Sitting on the stonework, fishing, was a species of kid whom I took to be Oswald the Plague-Spot.

Bingo was both surprised and delighted to see me, and introduced me to the kid. If the latter was surprised and delighted too, he concealed it like a diplomat. He just looked at me, raised his eyebrows slightly, and went on fishing. He was one of those supercilious striplings who give you the impression that you went to the wrong school and that your clothes don't fit.

'This is Oswald,' said Bingo.

'What,' I replied cordially, 'could be sweeter? How are you?'

'Oh, all right,' said the kid.

'Nice place, this.'

'Oh, all right,' said the kid.

'Having a good time fishing?'

'Oh, all right,' said the kid.

Young Bingo led me off to commune apart.

'Doesn't jolly old Oswald's incessant flow of prattle make your head ache sometimes?' I asked.

Bingo sighed.

'It's a hard job.'

'What's a hard job?'

'Loving him.'

'Do you love him?' I asked, surprised. I shouldn't have thought it could be done.

'I try to,' said young Bingo, 'for Her sake. She's coming back tomorrow, Bertie.'

'So I heard.'

'She is coming, my love, my own – '

'Absolutely,' I said. 'But touching on young Oswald

once more. Do you have to be with him all day? How do you manage to stick it?'

'Oh, he doesn't give much trouble. When we aren't working he sits on that bridge all the time, trying to catch tiddlers.'

'Why don't you shove him in?'

'Shove him in?'

'It seems to me distinctly the thing to do,' I said, regarding the stripling's back with a good deal of dislike. 'It would wake him up a bit, and make him take an interest in things.'

Bingo shook his head a bit wistfully.

'Your proposition attracts me,' he said, 'but I'm afraid it can't be done. You see, She would never forgive me. She is devoted to the little brute.'

'Great Scott!' I cried. 'I've got it!' I don't know if you know that feeling when you get an inspiration, and tingle all down your spine from the soft collar as now worn to the very soles of the old Waukeesis? Jeeves, I suppose, feels that way more or less all the time, but it isn't often it comes to me. But now all Nature seemed to be shouting at me. 'You've clicked!' and I grabbed young Bingo by the arm in a way that must have made him feel as if a horse had bitten him. His finely-chiselled features were twisted with agony and what not, and he asked me what the dickens I thought I was playing at.

'Bingo,' I said, 'what would Jeeves have done?'

'How do you mean, what would Jeeves have done?'

'I mean what would he have advised in a case like yours? I mean you wanting to make a hit with Honoria Glossop and all that. Why, take it from me, laddie, he would have shoved you behind that clump of bushes over there; he would have got me to lure Honoria on to the bridge somehow; then, at the proper time, he would have told me to give the kid a pretty hefty jab in the small of the back, so as to shoot him into the water; and then you would have dived in and hauled him out. How about it?'

'You didn't think that out by yourself, Bertie?' said young Bingo, in a hushed sort of voice.

'Yes, I did. Jeeves isn't the only fellow with ideas.'

'But it's absolutely wonderful.'

'Just a suggestion.'

'The only objection I can see is that it would be so dashed awkward for you. I mean to say, suppose the kid turned round and said you had shoved him in, that would make you frightfully unpopular with Her.'

'I don't mind risking that.'

The man was deeply moved.

'Bertie, this is noble.'

'No, no.'

He clasped my hand silently, then chuckled like the last drop of water going down the waste-pipe in a bath.

'Now what?' I said.

'I was only thinking,' said young Bingo, 'how fearfully wet Oswald will get. Oh, happy day!'

=3=
THE HERO'S REWARD

I don't know if you've noticed it, but it's rummy how nothing in this world ever seems to be absolutely perfect. The drawback to this otherwise singularly fruity binge was, of course, the fact that Jeeves wouldn't be on the spot to watch me in action. Still, apart from that there wasn't a flaw. The beauty of the thing was, you see, that nothing could possibly go wrong. You know how it is, as a rule, when you want to get Chappie A on Spot B at exactly the same moment when Chappie C is on Spot D. There's always a chance of a hitch. Take the case of a general, I mean to say, who's planning out a big movement. He tells one regiment to capture the hill with the windmill on it at the exact moment when another regiment is taking the bridgehead or something down in the valley; and everything gets all messed up. And then, when they're chatting the thing over in camp that night, the colonel of the first regiment says, "Oh, sorry! Did you say the hill with the windmill? I thought you said the one with the flock of sheep." And there you are! But in this case, nothing like that could happen, because Oswald and Bingo would be on the spot right along, so that all I had to worry about was getting Honoria there in due season. And I managed that all right, first shot, by asking her if she would come for a stroll in the grounds with me, as I had something particular to say to her.

She had arrived shortly after lunch in the car with

the Braythwayt girl. I was introduced to the latter, a tallish girl with blue eyes and fair hair. I rather took to her – she was so unlike Honoria – and, if I had been able to spare the time, I shouldn't have minded talking to her for a bit. But business was business – I had fixed it up with Bingo to be behind the bushes at three sharp, so I got hold of Honoria and steered her out through the grounds in the direction of the lake.

'You're very quiet, Mr Wooster,' she said.

Made me jump a bit. I was concentrating pretty tensely at the moment. We had just come in sight of the lake, and I was casting a keen eye over the ground to see that everything was in order. Everything appeared to be as arranged. The kid Oswald was hunched up on the bridge; and, as Bingo wasn't visible, I took it that he had got into position. My watch made it two minutes after the hour.

'Eh?' I said. 'Oh, ah, yes. I was just thinking.'

'You said you had something important to say to me.'

'Absolutely!' I had decided to open the proceedings by sort of paving the way for young Bingo. I mean to say, without actually mentioning his name, I wanted to prepare the girl's mind for the fact that, surprising as it might seem, there was someone who had long loved her from afar and all that sort of rot. 'It's like this,' I said. 'It may sound rummy and all that, but there's somebody who's frightfully in love with you and so forth – a friend of mine, you know.'

'Oh, a friend of yours?'

'Yes.'

She gave a kind of a laugh.

'Well, why doesn't he tell me so?'

'Well, you see, that's the sort of chap he is. Kind of shrinking, diffident kind of fellow. Hasn't got the nerve.

40

Thinks you so much above him, don't you know. Looks on you as a sort of goddess. Worships the ground you tread on, but can't whack up the ginger to tell you so.'

'This is very interesting.'

'Yes. He's not a bad chap, you know, in his way. Rather an ass, perhaps, but well-meaning. Well, that's the posish. You might just bear it in mind, what?'

'How funny you are!'

She chucked back her head and laughed with considerable vim. She had a penetrating sort of laugh. Rather like a train going into a tunnel. It didn't sound over-musical to me, and on the kid Oswald it appeared to jar not a little. He gazed at us with a good deal of dislike.

'I wish the dickens you wouldn't make that row,' he said. 'Scaring all the fish away.'

It broke the spell a bit. Honoria changed the subject.

'I do wish Oswald wouldn't sit on the bridge like that,' she said. 'I'm sure it isn't safe. He might easily fall in.'

'I'll go and tell him,' I said.

I suppose the distance between the kid and me at this juncture was about five yards, but I got the impression that it was nearer a hundred. And, as I started to toddle across the intervening space, I had a rummy feeling that I'd done this very thing before. Then I remembered. Years ago, at a country-house party, I had been roped in to play the part of a butler in some amateur theatricals in aid of some ghastly charity or other; and I had had to open the proceedings by walking across the empty stage from left upper entrance and shoving a tray on a table down right. They had impressed it on me at rehearsals that I mustn't take the course at a quick heel-and-toe, like a chappie finishing strongly in a walking-race; and the result was that I kept the brakes on to such an extent that it seemed to me as if I was never going to get to the bally table at all. The stage seemed to stretch out in front of me like a trackless desert, and there was a kind of breathless hush as if all Nature had paused to concentrate its attention on me personally. Well, I felt just like that now. I had a kind of dry gulping in my throat, and the more I walked the farther away the kid seemed to get, till suddenly I found myself standing just behind him without quite knowing how I'd got there.

'Hallo!' I said, with a sickly sort of grin – wasted on the kid, because he didn't bother to turn round and look at me. He merely wiggled his left ear in a rather peevish manner. I don't know when I've met anybody in whose life I appeared to mean so little.

'Hallo!' I said. 'Fishing?'

I laid my hand in a sort of elderly-brotherly way on his shoulder.

'Here, look out!' said the kid, wobbling on his foundations.

It was one of those things that want doing quickly or not at all. I shut my eyes and pushed. Something seemed to give. There was a scrambling sound, a kind of yelp, a scream in the offing, and a splash. And so the long day wore on, so to speak.

I opened my eyes. The kid was just coming to the surface.

'Help!' I shouted, cocking an eye on the bush from which young Bingo was scheduled to emerge.

Nothing happened. Young Bingo didn't emerge to the slightest extent whatever.

'I say! Help!' I shouted again.

I don't want to bore you with reminiscences of my theatrical career, but I must touch once more on that appearance of mine as the butler. The scheme on that occasion had been that when I put the tray on the table the heroine would come on and say a few words to get me off. Well, on the night the misguided female forgot to stand by, and it was a full minute before the search-party located her and shot her on to the stage. And all that time I had to stand there, waiting. A rotten sensation, believe me, and this was just the same, only worse. I understood what these writer-chappies mean when they talk about time standing still.

Meanwhile, the kid Oswald was presumably being cut off in his prime, and it began to seem to me that some sort of steps ought to be taken about it. What I had seen of the lad hadn't particularly endeared him to me, but it was undoubtedly a bit thick to let him pass away. I don't know when I have seen anything more grubby and unpleasant than the lake as viewed from the bridge; but the thing apparently had to be done. I chucked off my coat and vaulted over.

It seems rummy that water should be so much wetter when you go into it with your clothes on than when you're just bathing, but take it from me that it is. I was only under about three seconds, I suppose, but I came up feeling like the bodies you read of in the paper which "had evidently been in the water several days". I felt clammy and bloated.

At this point the scenario struck another snag. I had assumed that directly I came to the surface I should get hold of the kid and steer him courageously to shore. But he hadn't waited to be steered. When I had finished getting the water out of my eyes and had time to look round, I saw him about ten yards away, going strongly and using, I think, the Australian crawl. The spectacle took all the heart out of me. I mean to say, the whole essence of rescue, if you know what I mean, is that the party of the second part shall keep fairly still and in one spot. If he starts swimming off on his own account and can obviously give you at least forty yards in the hundred, where are you? The whole thing falls through. It didn't seem to me that there was much to be done except get ashore, so I got ashore. By the time I had landed, the kid was half-way to the house. Look at it from whatever angle you like, the thing was a wash-out.

I was interrupted in my meditations by a noise like the Scotch express going under a bridge. It was Honoria Glossop laughing. She was standing at my elbow, looking at me in a rummy manner.

'Oh, Bertie, you are funny!' she said. And even in that moment there seemed to me something sinister in the words. She had never called me anything except "Mr Wooster" before. 'How wet you are!'

'Yes, I am wet.'

'You had better hurry into the house and change.'

'Yes.'

I wrung a gallon or two of water out of my clothes.

'You *are* funny!' she said again. 'First proposing in that extraordinary roundabout way, and then pushing poor little Oswald into the lake so as to impress me by saving him.'

I managed to get the water out of my throat sufficiently to try to correct this fearful impression.

'No, no!'

'He said you pushed him in, and I saw you do it. Oh, I'm not angry, Bertie. I think it was too sweet of you. But I'm quite sure it's time that I took you in hand. You certainly want someone to look after you. You've been seeing too many moving-pictures. I suppose the next thing you would have done would have been to set the house on fire so as to rescue me.' She looked at me in a proprietary sort of way. 'I think,' she said, 'I shall be able to make something of you, Bertie. It is true yours has been a wasted life up to the present, but you are still young, and there is a lot of good in you.'

'No, really there isn't.'

'Oh, yes, there is. It simply wants bringing out. Now you run straight up to the house and change your wet clothes, or you will catch cold.'

And, if you know what I mean, there was a sort of motherly note in her voice which seemed to tell me, even more than her actual words, that I was for it.

As I was coming downstairs after changing, I ran into young Bingo, looking festive to a degree.

'Bertie!' he said. 'Just the man I wanted to see. Bertie, a wonderful thing has happened.'

'You blighter!' I cried. 'What became of you? Do you know -?'

'Oh, you mean about being in those bushes? I hadn't time to tell you about that. It's all off.'

'All off?'

'Bertie, I was actually starting to hide in those bushes when the most extraordinary thing happened. Walking across the lawn I saw the most radiant, the most beautiful girl in the world. There is none like her, none. Bertie, do you believe in love at first sight? You do believe in love at first sight, don't you, Bertie, old man? Directly I saw her she seemed to draw me like a magnet. I seemed to forget everything. We two were alone in a world of music and sunshine. I joined her. I got into conversation. She is a Miss Braythwayt, Bertie – Daphne Braythwayt. Directly our eyes met, I realized that what I had imagined to be my love for Honoria Glossop had been a mere passing whim. Bertie, you do believe in love at first sight, don't you? She is so wonderful, so sympathetic. Like a tender goddess – '

At this point I left the blighter.

Two days later I got a letter from Jeeves.

'. . . The weather,' it ended, 'continues fine. I have had one exceedingly enjoyable bathe.'

I gave one of those hollow, mirthless laughs, and went downstairs to join Honoria. I had an appointment with her in the drawing-room. She was going to read Ruskin to me.

=4=
INTRODUCING CLAUDE AND EUSTACE

The blow fell precisely at one forty-five (summer time). Spenser, Aunt Agatha's butler, was offering me the fried potatoes at the moment, and such was my emotion that I lofted six of them on to the sideboard with the spoon. Shaken to the core, if you know what I mean.

Mark you, I was in a pretty enfeebled condition already. I had been engaged to Honoria Glossop nearly two weeks, and during all that time not a day had passed without her putting in some heavy work in the direction of what Aunt Agatha had called "moulding" me. I had read solid literature till my eyes bubbled; we had legged it together through miles of picture-galleries; and I had been compelled to undergo classical concerts to an extent you would hardly believe. All in all, therefore, I was in no fit state to receive shocks, especially shocks like this. Honoria had lugged me round to lunch at Aunt Agatha's, and I had just been saying to myself, "Death, where is thy jolly old sting?" when she hove the bomb.

'Bertie,' she said, suddenly, as if she had just remembered it, 'what is the name of that man of yours — your valet?'

'Eh? Oh, Jeeves.'

'I think he's a bad influence for you,' said Honoria. 'When we are married, you must get rid of Jeeves.'

It was at this point that I jerked the spoon and sent six of the best and crispest sailing on to the sideboard, with Spenser gambolling after them like a dignified old retriever.

'Get rid of Jeeves!' I gasped.

'Yes. I don't like him.'

'*I* don't like him,' said Aunt Agatha.

'But I can't. I mean – why, I couldn't carry on for a day without Jeeves.'

'You will have to,' said Honoria. 'I don't like him at all.'

'*I* don't like him at all,' said Aunt Agatha. 'I never did.'

Ghastly, what? I'd always had an idea that marriage was a bit of a wash-out, but I'd never dreamed that it demanded such frightful sacrifices from a fellow. I passed the rest of the meal in a sort of stupor.

The scheme had been, if I remember, that after lunch I should go off and caddy for Honoria on a shopping tour down Regent Street; but when she got up and started collecting me and the rest of things, Aunt Agatha stopped her.

'You run along dear,' she said. 'I want to say a few words to Bertie.'

So Honoria legged it, and Aunt Agatha drew up her chair and started in.

'Bertie,' she said, 'dear Honoria does not know it, but a little difficulty has arisen about your marriage.'

'By Jove! not really?' I said, hope starting to dawn.

'Oh, it's nothing at all, of course. It is only a little exasperating. The fact is, Sir Roderick is being rather troublesome.'

'Thinks I'm not a good bet? Wants to scratch the fixture? Well, perhaps he's right.'

'Pray do not be so absurd, Bertie. It is nothing so

48

serious as that. But the nature of Sir Roderick's profession unfortunately makes him – over-cautious.'

I didn't get it.

'Over-cautious?'

'Yes. I suppose it is inevitable. A nerve specialist with his extensive practice can hardly help taking a rather warped view of humanity.'

I got what she was driving at now. Sir Roderick Glossop, Honoria's father, is always called a nerve specialist, because it sounds better, but everybody knows that he's really a sort of janitor to the looney-bin. I mean to say, when your uncle the Duke begins to feel the strain a bit and you find him in the blue drawing-room sticking straws in his hair, old Glossop is the first person you send for. He toddles round, gives the patient the once-over, talks about over-excited nervous systems, and recommends complete rest and seclusion and all that sort of thing. Practically every posh family in the country has called him in at one time or another, and I suppose that, being in that position – I mean constantly having to sit on people's heads while their nearest and dearest phone to the asylum to send round the wagon – does tend to make a chappie take what you might call a warped view of humanity.

'You mean he thinks I may be a looney, and he doesn't want a looney son-in-law?' I said.

Aunt Agatha seemed rather peeved than otherwise at my deadly intelligence.

'Of course, he does not think anything so ridiculous. I told you he was simply exceedingly cautious. He wants to satisfy himself that you are perfectly normal.' Here she paused, for Spenser had come in with the coffee. When he had gone, she went on: 'He appears to have got hold of some extraordinary story about your having pushed his son Oswald into the lake at Ditteredge Hall.

Incredible, of course. Even you would hardly do a thing like that.'

'Well, I did sort of lean against him, you know, and he shot off the bridge.'

'Oswald definitely accuses you of having pushed him into the water. That has disturbed Sir Roderick, and unfortunately it has caused him to make inquiries, and he has heard about your poor Uncle Henry.'

She eyed me with a good deal of solemnity, and I took a grave sip of coffee. We were peeping into the family cupboard and having a look at the good old skeleton. My late Uncle Henry, you see, was by way of being the blot on the Wooster escutcheon. An extremely decent chappie personally, and one who had always endeared himself to me by tipping me with considerable lavishness when I was at school; but there's no doubt he did at times do rather rummy things, notably keeping eleven pet rabbits in his bedroom; and I suppose a purist might have considered him more or less off his onion. In fact, to be perfectly frank, he wound up his career, happy to the last and completely surrounded by rabbits, in some sort of a home.

'It is very absurd, of course,' continued Aunt Agatha. 'If any of the family had inherited poor Henry's eccentricity – and it was nothing more – it would have been Claude and Eustace, and there could not be two brighter boys.'

Claude and Eustace were twins, and had been kids at school with me in my last summer term. Casting my mind back, it seemed to me that "bright" just about described them. The whole of that term, as I remembered it, had been spent in getting them out of a series of frightful rows.

'Look how well they are doing at Oxford. Your Aunt Emily had a letter from Claude only the other day saying that they hoped to be elected shortly to a very important college club, called The Seekers.'

'Seekers?' I couldn't recall any club of the name in my time at Oxford. 'What do they seek?'

'Claude did not say. Truth or knowledge, I should imagine. It is evidently a very desirable club to belong to, for Claude added that Lord Rainsby, the Earl of Datchet's son, was one of his fellow-candidates. However, we are wandering from the point, which is that Sir Roderick wants to have a quiet talk with you quite alone. Now I rely on you, Bertie, to be — I won't say intelligent, but at least sensible. Don't giggle nervously; try to keep that horrible glassy expression out of your eyes: don't yawn or fidget; and remember that Sir Roderick is the president of the West London branch of the anti-gambling league, so please do not talk about horse-racing. He will lunch with you at your flat tomorrow at one-thirty. Please remember that he drinks no wine, strongly disapproves of smoking, and can only eat the simplest food, owing to an impaired digestion. Do not offer him coffee, for he considers it the root of half the nerve-trouble in the world.'

'I should think a dog-biscuit and a glass of water would about meet the case, what?'

'Bertie!'

'Oh, all right. Merely persiflage.'

'Now it is precisely that sort of idiotic remark that would be calculated to arouse Sir Roderick's worst suspicions. Do please try to refrain from any misguided flippancy when you are with him. He is a very serious-minded man . . . Are you going? Well, please remember all I have said. I rely on you, and, if anything goes wrong, I shall never forgive you.'

'Right-o!' I said.

And so home, with a jolly day to look forward to.

I breakfasted pretty late next morning and went for a stroll afterwards. It seemed to me that anything I could do to clear the old lemon ought to be done, and a bit of fresh air generally relieves that rather foggy feeling that comes over a fellow early in the day. I had taken a stroll in the park, and got back as far as Hyde Park Corner, when some blighter sloshed me between the shoulder-blades. It was young Eustace, my cousin. He was arm-in-arm with two other fellows, the one on the outside being my cousin Claude and the one in the middle a pink-faced chappie with light hair and an apologetic sort of look.

'Bertie, old egg!' said Eustace affably.

'Hallo!' I said, not frightfully chirpily.

'Fancy running into you, the one man in London who can support us in the style we are accustomed to! By the way, you've never met old Dog-Face, have you? Dog-Face, this is my cousin Bertie. Lord Rainsby – Mr Wooster. We've just been round to your flat, Bertie. Bitterly disappointed that you were out, but were hospitably entertained by old Jeeves. That man's a corker, Bertie. Stick to him.'

'What are you doing in London?' I asked.

'Oh, buzzing round. We're just up for the day. Flying visit, strictly unofficial. We oil back on the three-ten. And now, touching that lunch you very decently volunteered to stand us, which shall it be? Ritz? Savoy? Carlton? Or, if you're a member of Ciro's or the Embassy, that would do just as well.'

'I can't give you lunch. I've got an engagement myself. And, by Jove,' I said, taking a look at my watch, 'I'm late.' I hailed a taxi. 'Sorry.'

'As man to man, then,' said Eustace, 'lend us a fiver.'

I hadn't time to stop and argue. I unbelted the fiver and hopped into the cab. It was twenty to two when I got to the flat. I bounded into the sitting-room, but it was empty.

Jeeves shimmied in.

'Sir Roderick has not yet arrived, sir.'

'Good egg!' I said. 'I thought I should find him smashing up the furniture.' My experience is that the less you want a fellow, the more punctual he's bound to be, and I had had a vision of the old lad pacing the rug in my sitting-room, saying "He cometh not!" and generally hotting up. 'Is everything in order?'

'I fancy you will find the arrangements quite satisfactory, sir.'

'What are you giving us?'

'Cold consommé, a cutlet, and a savoury, sir. With lemon-squash, iced.'

'Well, I don't see how that can hurt him. Don't go getting carried away by the excitement of the thing and start bringing in coffee.'

'No, sir.'

'And don't let your eyes get glassy, because, if you do, you're apt to find yourself in a padded cell before you know where you are.'

'Very good, sir.'

There was a ring at the bell.

'Stand by, Jeeves,' I said. 'We're off!'

=5=
SIR RODERICK COMES TO LUNCH

I had met Sir Roderick Glossop before, of course, but only when I was with Honoria; and there is something about Honoria which makes almost anybody you meet in the same room seem sort of under-sized and trivial by comparison. I had never realized till this moment what an extraordinarily formidable old bird he was. He had a pair of shaggy eyebrows which gave his eyes a piercing look which was not at all the sort of thing a fellow wanted to encounter on an empty stomach. He was fairly tall and fairly broad, and he had the most enormous head, with practically no hair on it, which made it seem bigger and much more like the dome of St Paul's. I suppose he must have taken about a nine or something in hats. Shows what a rotten thing it is to let your brain develop too much.

'What ho! What ho! What ho!' I said, trying to strike the genial note, and then had a sudden feeling that that was just the sort of thing I had been warned not to say. Dashed difficult it is to start things going properly on an occasion like this. A fellow living in a London flat is so handicapped. I mean to say, if I had been the young squire greeting the visitor in the country, I could have said, "Welcome to Meadowsweet Hall!" or something zippy like that. It sounds silly to say "Welcome to Number 6A, Crichton Mansions, Berkeley Street, W."

'I am afraid I am a little late,' he said as we sat down. 'I was detained at my club by Lord Alastair Hungerford, the Duke of Ramfurline's son. His Grace, he informed me, had exhibited a renewal of the symptons which have been causing the family so much concern. I could not leave him immediately. Hence my unpunctuality, which I trust has not discommoded you.'

'Oh, not at all. So the Duke is off his rocker, what?'

'The expression which you use is not precisely the one I should have employed myself with reference to the head of perhaps the noblest family in England, but there is no doubt that cerebral excitement does, as you suggest, exist in no small degree.' He sighed as well as he could with his mouth full of cutlet. 'A profession like mine is a great strain, a great strain.'

'Must be.'

'Sometimes I am appalled at what I see around me.' He stopped suddenly and sort of stiffened. 'Do you keep a cat, Mr Wooster?'

'Eh? What? Cat? No, no cat.'

'I was conscious of a distinct impression that I had heard a cat mewing either in the room or very near to where we are sitting.'

'Probably a taxi or something in the street.'

'I fear I do not follow you.'

'I mean to say, taxis squawk, you know. Rather like cats in a sort of way.'

'I had not observed the resemblance,' he said, rather coldly.

'Have some lemon-squash,' I said. The conversation seemed to be getting rather difficult.

'Thank you. Half a glassful, if I may.' The hell-brew appeared to buck him up, for he resumed in a slightly more pally manner. 'I have a particular dislike for cats. But I was saying – Oh, yes. Sometimes I am positively appalled at what I see around me. It is not only the cases which come under my professional notice, painful as many of those are. It is what I see as I go about London. Sometimes it seems to me that the whole world is mentally unbalanced. This very morning, for example, a most singular and distressing occurrence took place as I was driving from my house to the club. The day being clement, I had instructed my chauffeur to open my landaulette, and I was leaning back, deriving no little pleasure from the sunshine, when our progress was arrested in the middle of the thoroughfare by one of those blocks in the traffic which are inevitable in so congested a system as that of London.'

I suppose I had been letting my mind wander a bit, for when he stopped and took a sip of lemon-squash I had a feeling that I was listening to a lecture and was expected to say something.

'Hear, hear!' I said.

'I beg your pardon?'

'Nothing, nothing. You were saying – '

'The vehicles proceeding in the opposite direction had also been temporarily arrested, but after a moment they were permitted to proceed. I had fallen into a meditation, when suddenly the most extraordinary thing took place. My hat was snatched abruptly from my head! And as I looked back I perceived it being waved in a kind of feverish triumph from the interior of a taxicab, which, even as I looked, disappeared through a gap in the traffic and was lost to sight.'

I didn't laugh, but I distinctly heard a couple of my floating ribs part from their moorings under the strain.

'Must have been meant for a practical joke,' I said. 'What?'

This suggestion didn't seem to please the old boy.

'I trust,' he said, 'I am not deficient in an appreciation

of the humorous, but I confess that I am at a loss to detect anything akin to pleasantry in the outrage. The action was beyond all question that of a mentally unbalanced subject. These mental lesions may express themselves in almost any form. The Duke of Ramfurline, to whom I had occasion to allude just now, is under the impression – this is in the strictest confidence – that he is a canary: and his seizure today, which so perturbed Lord Alastair, was due to the fact that a careless footman had neglected to bring him his morning lump of sugar. Cases are common, again, of men waylaying women and cutting off portions of their hair. It is from a branch of this latter form of mania that I should be disposed to imagine that my assailant was suffering. I can only trust that he will be placed under proper control before he – Mr Wooster, there *is* a cat closer at hand! It is *not* in the street! The mewing appears to come from the adjoining room.'

This time I had to admit there was no doubt about it. There was a distinct sound of mewing coming from the next room. I punched the bell for Jeeves, who drifted in and stood waiting with an air of respectful devotion.

'Sir?'

'Oh, Jeeves,' I said. 'Cats! What about it? Are there any cats in the flat?'

'Only the three in your bedroom, sir.'

'What!'

'Cats in his bedroom!' I heard Sir Roderick whisper in a kind of stricken way, and his eyes hit me amidships like a couple of bullets.

'What do you mean,' I said, 'only the three in my bedroom?'

'The black one, the tabby and the small lemon-coloured animal, sir.'

'What on earth – ?'

I charged round the table in the direction of the door. Unfortunately, Sir Roderick had just decided to edge in that direction himself, with the result that we collided in the doorway with a good deal of force, and staggered out into the hall together. He came smartly out of the clinch and grabbed an umbrella from the rack.

'Stand back!' he shouted, waving it overhead. 'Stand back, sir! I am armed!'

It seemed to me that the moment had come to be soothing.

'Awfully sorry I barged into you,' I said. 'Wouldn't have had it happen for worlds. I was just dashing out to have a look into things.'

He appeared a trifle reassured, and lowered the umbrella. But just then the most frightful shindy started in the bedroom. It sounded as though all the cats in London, assisted by delegates from outlying suburbs, had got together to settle their differences once for all. A sort of augmented orchestra of cats.

'This noise is unendurable,' yelled Sir Roderick. 'I cannot hear myself speak.'

'I fancy, sir,' said Jeeves respectfully, 'that the animals may have become somewhat exhilarated as the result of having discovered the fish under Mr Wooster's bed.'

The old boy tottered.

'Fish! Did I hear you rightly?'

'Sir?'

'Did you say that there was a fish under Mr Wooster's bed?'

'Yes, sir.'

Sir Roderick gave a low moan, and reached for his hat and stick.

'You aren't going?' I said.

'Mr Wooster, I *am* going! I prefer to spend my leisure time in less eccentric society.'

'But I say. Here, I must come with you. I'm sure the whole business can be explained. Jeeves, my hat.'

Jeeves rallied round. I took the hat from him and shoved it on my head.

'Good heavens!'

Beastly shock it was! The bally thing had absolutely engulfed me, if you know what I mean. Even as I was putting it on I got a sort of impression that it was a trifle roomy; and no sooner had I let it go than it settled down over my ears like a kind of extinguisher.

'I say! This isn't my hat!'

'It is *my* hat!' said Sir Roderick in about the coldest, nastiest voice I'd ever heard. 'The hat which was stolen from me this morning as I drove in my car.'

'But – '

I suppose Napoleon or somebody like that would have been equal to the situation, but I'm bound to say it was too much for me. I just stood there goggling in a sort of coma, while the old boy lifted the hat off me and turned to Jeeves.

'I should be glad, my man,' he said, 'if you would accompany me a few yards down the street. I wish to ask you some questions.'

'Very good, sir.'

'Here, but, I say – !' I began, but he left me standing. He stalked out, followed by Jeeves. And at that moment the row in the bedroom started again, louder than ever.

I was about fed up with the whole thing. I mean, cats in your bedroom – a bit thick, what? I didn't know how the dickens they had got in, but I was jolly well resolved that they weren't going to stay picnicking there any longer. I flung open the door. I got a momentary flash of about a hundred and fifteen cats of all sizes and colours scrapping in the middle of the room, and then they all shot past me with a rush and out of the front door; and all that was left of the mob-scene was the head of a whacking big fish, lying on the carpet and staring up at me in a rather austere sort of way, as if it wanted a written explanation and apology.

There was something about the thing's expression that absolutely chilled me, and I withdrew on tiptoe and shut the door. And, as I did so, I bumped into someone.

'Oh, sorry!' he said.

I spun round. It was the pink-faced chappie, Lord Something or other, the fellow I had met with Claude and Eustace.

'I say,' he said apologetically, 'awfully sorry to bother you, but those weren't my cats I met just now legging it downstairs, were they? They looked like my cats.'

'They came out of my bedroom.'

'Then they *were* my cats!' he said sadly. 'Oh, dash it!'

'Did you put cats in my bedroom?'

'Your man, what's-his-name, did. He rather decently said I could keep them there till my train went. I'd just come to fetch them. And now they've gone! Oh, well, it can't be helped, I suppose. I'll take the hat and the fish, anyway.'

I was beginning to dislike this chappie.

'Did you put that bally fish there, too?'

'No, that was Eustace's. The hat was Claude's.'

I sank limply into a chair.

'I say, you couldn't explain this, could you?' I said. The chappie gazed at me in mild surprise.

'Why, don't you know all about it? I say!' He blushed profusely. 'Why, if you don't know about it, I shouldn't wonder if the whole thing didn't seem rummy to you.'

'Rummy is the word.'

'It was for The Seekers, you know?'

'The Seekers?'

'Rather a blood club, you know, up at Oxford, which your cousins and I are rather keen on getting into. You have to pinch something, you know, to get elected. Some sort of a souvenir, you know. A policeman's helmet, you know, or a door-knocker or something, you know. The room's decorated with the things at the annual dinner, and everybody makes speeches and all that sort of thing. Rather jolly! Well, we wanted rather to make a sort of special effort and do the thing in style, if you understand, so we came up to London to see if we couldn't pick up something here that would be a bit out of the ordinary. And we had the most amazing luck right from the start. Your cousin Claude managed to collect a quite decent top-hat out of a passing car and your cousin Eustace got away with a really goodish salmon or something from Harrods, and I snaffled three excellent cats all in the first hour. We were fearfully braced, I can tell you. And then the difficulty was to know where to park the things till our train went. You look so beastly conspicuous, you know, tooling about London with a fish and a lot of cats. And then Eustace remembered you, and we all came on here in a cab. You were out, but your man said it would be all right. When we met you, you were in such a hurry that we hadn't time to explain. Well, I think I'll be taking the hat, if you don't mind.'

'It's gone.'

'Gone?'

'The fellow you pinched it from happened to be the man who was lunching here. He took it away with him.'

61

'Oh, I say! Poor old Claude will be upset. Well, how about the goodish salmon or something?'

'Would you care to view the remains?' He seemed all broken up when he saw the wreckage.

'I doubt if the committee would accept that,' he said sadly. 'There isn't a frightful lot of it left, what?'

'The cats ate the rest.'

He sighed deeply.

'No cats, no fish, no hat. We've had all our trouble for nothing. I do call that hard! And on top of that – I say, I hate to ask you, but you couldn't lend me a tenner, could you?'

'A tenner? What for?'

'Well, the fact is, I've got to pop round and bail Claude and Eustace out. They've been arrested.'

'Arrested!'

'Yes. You see, what with the excitement of collaring the hat and the salmon or something, added to the fact that we had rather a festive lunch, they got a bit above themselves, poor chaps, and tried to pinch a motor-lorry. Silly, of course, because I don't see how they could have got the thing to Oxford and shown it to the committee. Still, there wasn't any reasoning with them, and when the driver started making a fuss, there was a bit of a mix-up, and Claude and Eustace are more or less languishing in Vine Street police-station till I pop round and bail them out. So if you could manage a tenner – Oh, thanks, that's fearfully good of you. It would have been too bad to leave them there, what? I mean, they're both such frightfully good chaps, you know. Everybody likes them up at the Varsity. They're fearfully popular.'

'I bet they are!' I said.

When Jeeves came back, I was waiting for him on the mat. I wanted speech with the blighter.

'Well?' I said.

'Sir Roderick asked me a number of questions, sir, respecting your habits and mode of life, to which I replied guardedly.'

'I don't care about that. What I want to know is why you didn't explain the whole thing to him right at the start? A word from you would have put everything clear.'

'Yes, sir.'

'Now he's gone off thinking me a looney.'

'I should not be surprised, from his conversation with me, sir, if some such idea had not entered his head.'

I was just starting in to speak, when the telephone bell rang. Jeeves answered it.

'No, madam, Mr Wooster is not in. No, madam, I do not know when he will return. No, madam, he left no message. Yes, madam, I will inform him.' He put back the receiver. 'Mrs Gregson, sir.'

Aunt Agatha! I had been expecting it. Ever since the luncheon-party had blown out a fuse, her shadow had been hanging over me, so to speak.

'Does she know? Already?'

'I gather that Sir Roderick has been speaking to her on the telephone, sir, and – '

'No wedding bells for me, what?'

Jeeves coughed.

'Mrs Gregson did not actually confide in me, sir, but I fancy that some such thing may have occurred. She seemed decidedly agitated, sir.'

It's a rummy thing, but I'd been so snootered by the old boy and the cats and the fish and the hat and the pink-faced chappie and all the rest of it that the bright side simply hadn't occurred to me till now. By Jove, it was like a bally weight rolling off my chest! I gave a yelp of pure relief.

'Jeeves!' I said, 'I believe you worked the whole thing!'

'Sir?'

'I believe you had the jolly old situation in hand right from the start.'

'Well, sir, Spenser, Mrs Gregson's butler, who inadvertently chanced to overhear something of your conversation when you were lunching at the house, did mention certain of the details to me; and I confess that, though it may be a liberty to say so, I entertained hopes that something might occur to prevent the match. I doubt if the young lady was entirely suitable to you, sir.'

'And she would have shot you out on your ear five minutes after the ceremony.'

'Yes, sir. Spenser informed me that she had expressed some such intention. Mrs Gregson wishes you to call upon her immediately, sir.'

'She does, eh? What do you advise, Jeeves?'

'I think a trip abroad might prove enjoyable, sir.'

I shook my head. 'She'd come after me.'

'Not if you went far enough afield sir. There are excellent boats leaving every Wednesday and Saturday for New York.'

'Jeeves,' I said, 'you are right, as always. Book the tickets.'

=6=
JEEVES AND THE YULE-TIDE SPIRIT

The letter arrived on the morning of the sixteenth. I was pushing a bit of breakfast into the Wooster face at the moment and, feeling fairly well-fortified with coffee and kippers, I decided to break the news to Jeeves without delay. As Shakespeare says, if you're going to do a thing you might just as well pop right at it and get it over. The man would be disappointed, of course, and possibly even chagrined: but, dash it all, a splash of disappointment here and there does a fellow good. Makes him realize that life is stern and life is earnest.

'Oh, Jeeves,' I said.

'Sir?'

'We have here a communication from Lady Wickham. She has written inviting me to Skeldings for the festives. So you will see about bunging the necessaries together. We repair thither on the twenty-third. Plenty of white ties, Jeeves, also a few hearty country suits for use in the daytime. We shall be there some little time, I expect.'

There was a pause. I could feel he was directing a frosty gaze at me, but I dug into the marmalade and refused to meet it.

'I thought I understood you to say, sir, that you proposed to visit Monte Carlo immediately after Christmas.'

'I know. But that's all off. Plans changed.'

'Very good, sir.'

At this point the telephone bell rang, tiding over very nicely what had threatened to be an awkward moment. Jeeves unhooked the receiver.

'Yes? . . . Yes, madam . . . Very good, madam. Here is Mr Wooster.' He handed me the instrument. 'Mrs Spenser Gregson, sir.'

You know, every now and then I can't help feeling that Jeeves is losing his grip. In his prime it would have been with him the work of a moment to have told Aunt Agatha that I was not at home. I gave him one of those reproachful glances, and took the machine.

'Hullo?' I said. 'Yes? Hullo? Hullo? Bertie speaking. Hullo? Hullo? Hullo?'

'Don't keep on saying Hullo,' yipped the old relative in her customary curt manner. 'You're not a parrot. Sometimes I wish you were, because then you might have a little sense.'

Quite the wrong sort of tone to adopt towards a fellow in the early morning, of course, but what can one do?

'Bertie, Lady Wickham tells me she has invited you to Skeldings for Christmas. Are you going?'

'Rather!'

'Well, mind you behave yourself. Lady Wickham is an old friend of mine.'

I was in no mood for this sort of thing over the telephone. Face to face, I'm not saying, but at the end of a wire, no.

'I shall naturally endeavour, Aunt Agatha,' I replied stiffly, 'to conduct myself in a manner befitting an English gentleman paying a visit – '

'What did you say? Speak up. I can't hear.'

'I said Right-ho.'

'Oh? Well, mind you do. And there's another reason why I particularly wish you to be as little of an imbecile as you can manage while at Skeldings. Sir Roderick Glossop will be there.'

'What!'

'Don't bellow like that. You nearly deafened me.'

'Did you say Sir Roderick Glossop?'

'I did.'

'You don't mean Tuppy Glossop?'

'I mean Sir Roderick Glossop. Which was my reason for saying Sir Roderick Glossop. Now, Bertie, I want you to listen to me attentively. Are you there?'

'Yes, still here.'

'Well, then, listen. I have at last succeeded, after incredible difficulty, and in face of all the evidence, in almost persuading Sir Roderick that you are not actually insane. He is prepared to suspend judgment until he has seen you once more. On your behaviour at Skeldings, therefore – '

But I had hung up the receiver. Shaken. That's what I was. S. to the core.

Stop me if I've told you this before: but, in case you don't know, let me just mention the facts in the matter of this Glossop. He was a formidable old bird with a bald head and out-size eyebrows, by profession a looney-doctor. How it happened, I couldn't tell you to this day, but I once got engaged to his daughter, Honoria, a ghastly dynamic exhibit who read Nietzsche and had a laugh like waves breaking on a stern and rock-bound coast. The fixture was scratched owing to events occurring which convinced the old boy that I was off my napper; and since then he has always had my name at the top of his list of "Loonies I have Lunched With".

It seemed to me that even at Christmas time, with all the peace on earth and goodwill towards men that there is knocking about at that season, a reunion with this bloke was likely to be tough going. If I hadn't had more than one particularly good reason for wanting to go to Skeldings, I'd have called the thing off.

'Jeeves,' I said, all of a twitter. 'Do you know what? Sir Roderick Glossop is going to be at Lady Wickham's.'

'Very good, sir. If you have finished breakfast, I will clear away.'

Cold and haughty. No symp. None of the rallying-round spirit which one likes to see. As I had anticipated, the information that we were not going to Monte Carlo had got in amongst him. There is a keen sporting streak in Jeeves, and I knew he had been looking forward to a little flutter at the tables.

We Woosters can wear the mask. I ignored his lack of decent feeling.

'Do so Jeeves,' I said proudly, 'and with all convenient speed.'

Relations continued pretty fairly strained all through the rest of the week. There was a frigid detachment in the way the man brought me my dollop of tea in the mornings. Going down to Skeldings in the car on the afternoon of the twenty-third, he was aloof and reserved. And before dinner on the first night of my visit he put the studs in my dress-shirt in what I can only call a marked manner. The whole thing was extremely painful, and it seemed to me, as I lay in bed on the morning of the twenty-fourth, that the only step to take was to put the whole facts of the case before him and trust to his native good sense to effect an understanding.

I was feeling considerably in the pink that morning. Everything had gone like a breeze. My hostess, Lady Wickham, was a beaky female built far too closely on the lines of my Aunt Agatha for comfort, but she had seemed matey enough on my arrival. Her daughter, Roberta, had welcomed me with a warmth which, I'm bound to say, had set the old heart-strings fluttering a bit. And Sir Roderick, in the brief moment we had had together, appeared to have let the Yule-Tide Spirit soak into him to the most amazing extent. When he saw me, his mouth sort of flickered at one corner, which I took to be his idea of smiling, and he said, 'Ha, young man!' Not particularly chummily, but he said it: and my view was that it practically amounted to the lion lying down with the lamb.

So, all in all, life at this juncture seemed pretty well all to the mustard, and I decided to tell Jeeves exactly how matters stood.

'Jeeves,' I said, as he appeared with the steaming.

'Sir?'

'Touching on this business of our being here, I would like to say a few words of explanation. I consider that you have a right to the facts.'

'Sir?'

'I'm afraid scratching that Monte Carlo trip has been a bit of a jar for you, Jeeves.'

'Not at all, sir.'

'Oh, yes, it has. The heart was set on wintering in the world's good old Plague Spot. I know, I saw your eye light up when I said we were due for a visit there. You snorted a bit and your fingers twitched. I know, I know. And now that there has been a change of programme the iron has entered into your soul.'

'Not at all, sir.'

'Oh, yes, it has. I've seen it. Very well, then, what I wish to impress upon you, Jeeves, is that I have not been actuated in this matter by any mere idle whim. It was through no light and airy caprice that I accepted this invitation to Lady Wickham's. I have been angling for it for weeks, prompted by many considerations. In the first place, does one get the Yule-tide spirit at a spot like Monte Carlo?'

'Does one desire the Yule-tide spirit, sir?'

'Certainly one does. I am all for it. Well, that's one thing. Now here's another. It was imperative that I should come to Skeldings for Christmas, Jeeves, because I knew that young Tuppy Glossop was going to be here.'

'Sir Roderick Glossop, sir?'

'His nephew. You may have observed hanging about the place a fellow with light hair and a Cheshire-cat grin. That is Tuppy, and I have been anxious for some time to get to grips with him, I have it in for that man of wrath. Listen to the facts, Jeeves, and tell me if I am not justified in planning a hideous vengeance.' I took a sip of tea, for the mere memory of my wrongs had shaken me. 'In spite of the fact that young Tuppy is the nephew of Sir Roderick Glossop, at whose hands, Jeeves, as you are aware. I have suffered much, I fraternized with him freely, both at the Drones Club and elsewhere. I said to myself that a man is not to be blamed for his relations, and that I would hate to have my pals hold my Aunt Agatha, for instance, against me. Broad-minded, Jeeves, I think?'

'Extremely, sir.'

'Well, then, as I say, I sought this Tuppy out, Jeeves, and hobnobbed, and what do you think he did?'

'I could not say, sir.'

'I will tell you. One night after dinner at the Drones he betted me I wouldn't swing myself across the swimming-bath by the ropes and rings. I took him on and was buzzing along in great style until I came to the last ring. And then I found that this fiend in human shape had looped it back against the rail, thus leaving me hanging in the void with no means of getting ashore to my home and loved ones. There was nothing for it but to drop into the water. He told me that he had often caught fellows that way: and what I maintain, Jeeves, is that, if I can't get back at him somehow at Skeldings – with all the vast resources which a country-house affords at my disposal – I am not the man I was.'

'I see, sir.'

There was still something in his manner which told me that even now he lacked complete sympathy and understanding, so, delicate though the subject was, I decided to put all my cards on the table.

'And now, Jeeves, we came to the most important reason why I had to spend Christmas at Skeldings. Jeeves,' I said, diving into the old cup once more for a moment and bringing myself out wreathed in blushes, 'the fact of the matter is, I'm in love.'

'Indeed, sir?'

'You've seen Miss Roberta Wickham?'

'Yes, sir.'

'Very well, then.'

There was a pause, while I let it sink in.

'During your stay here, Jeeves,' I said, 'you will, no doubt, be thrown a good deal together with Miss Wickham's maid. On such occasions, pitch it strong.'

'Sir?'

'You know what I mean. Tell her that I'm rather a good chap. Mention my hidden depths. These things get round. Dwell on the fact that I have a kind heart and was runner-up in the Squash Handicap at the Drones this year. A boost is never wasted, Jeeves.'

'Very good, sir. But – '

'But what?'

'Well, sir – '

'I wish you wouldn't say "Well, sir" in that soupy

tone of voice. I have had to speak of this before. The habit is one that is growing upon you. Check it. What's on your mind?'

'I hardly like to take the liberty – '

'Carry on, Jeeves. We are always glad to hear from you, always.'

'What I was about to remark, if you will excuse me, sir, was that, I would scarcely have thought Miss Wickham a suitable – '

'Jeeves,' I said coldly, 'if you have anything to say against that lady, it had better not be said in my presence.'

'Very good, sir.'

'Or anywhere else, for that matter. What is your kick against Miss Wickham?'

'Oh, really, sir!'

'Jeeves, I insist. This is a time for plain speaking. You have beefed about Miss Wickham. I wish to know why.'

'It merely crossed my mind, sir, that for a gentlemen of your description Miss Wickham is not a suitable mate.'

'What do you mean by a gentleman of my description?'

'Well, sir – '

'Jeeves!'

'I beg your pardon, sir. The expression escaped me inadvertently. I was about to observe that I can only asseverate – '

'Only what?'

'I can only say that, as you have invited my opinion – '

'But I didn't.'

'I was under the impression that your desired to canvass my views on the matter, sir.'

'Oh? Well, let's have them anyway.'

72

'Very good, sir. Then briefly, if I may say so, sir, though Miss Wickham is a charming young lady – '

'There, Jeeves, you spoke an imperial quart. What eyes!'

'Yes, sir.'

'What hair!'

'Very true, sir.'

'And what *espièglerie*, if that's the word I want.'

'The exact word, sir.'

'All right, then. Carry on.'

'I grant Miss Wickham the possession of all these desirable qualities, sir. Nevertheless, considered as a matrimonial prospect for a gentleman of your description, I cannot look upon her as suitable. In my opinion Miss Wickham lacks seriousness, sir. She is too volatile and frivolous. To qualify as Miss Wickham's husband, a gentleman would need to possess a commanding personality and considerable strength of character.'

'Exactly!'

'I would always hesitate to recommend as a life's companion a young lady with quite such a vivid shade of red hair. Red hair, sir, in my opinion, is dangerous.'

I eyed the blighter squarely.

'Jeeves,' I said, 'you're talking rot.'

'Very good, sir.'

'Absolute drivel.'

'Very good, sir.'

'Pure mashed potatoes.'

'Very good, sir.'

'Very good, sir – I mean very good, Jeeves, that will be all,' I said.

And I drank a modicum of tea, with a good deal of hauteur.

It isn't often that I find myself able to prove Jeeves in

the wrong, but by dinner-time that night I was in a position to do so, and I did it without delay.

'Touching on that matter we were touching on, Jeeves,' I said, coming in from the bath and tackling him as he studied the shirt, 'I should be glad if you would give me your careful attention for a moment. I warn you that what I am about to say is going to make you look pretty silly.'

'Indeed, sir?'

'Yes, Jeeves. Pretty dashed silly it's going to make you look. It may lead you to be rather more careful in future about broadcasting these estimates of yours of people's characters. This morning, if I remember rightly, you stated that Miss Wickham was volatile, frivolous and lacking in seriousness. Am I correct?'

'Quite correct, sir.'

'Then what I have to tell you may cause you to alter that opinion. I went for a walk with Miss Wickham this afternoon: and, as we walked, I told her about what young Tuppy Glossop did to me in the swimming-bath at the Drones. She hung upon my words, Jeeves, and was full of sympathy.'

'Indeed, sir?'

'Dripping with it. And that's not all. Almost before I had finished, she was suggesting the ripest, fruitiest, brainiest scheme for bringing young Tuppy's grey hairs in sorrow to the grave that anyone could possibly imagine.'

'That is very gratifying, sir.'

'Gratifying is the word. It appears that at the girls' school where Miss Wickham was educated, Jeeves, it used to become necessary from time to time for the right-thinking element of the community to slip it across certain of the baser sort. Do you know what they did, Jeeves?'

'No, sir.'

'They took a long stick, Jeeves, and – follow me closely here – they tied a darning-needle to the end of it. Then at dead of night, it appears, they sneaked privily into the party of the second part's cubicle and shoved the needle through the bed-clothes and punctured her hot-water bottle. Girls are much subtler in these matters than boys, Jeeves. At my old school one would occasionally heave a jug of water over another bloke during the night-watches, but we never thought of effecting the same result in this particularly neat and scientific manner. Well, Jeeves, that was the scheme which Miss Wickham suggested I should work on young Tuppy, and this is the girl you call frivolous and lacking in seriousness. Any girl who can think up a wheeze like that is my idea of a helpmeet. I shall be glad, Jeeves, if by the time I came to bed to-night you have for me in this room a stout stick with a good sharp darning-needle attached.'

'Well, sir – '

I raised my hand.

'Jeeves,' I said. 'Not another word. Stick, one, and needle, darning, good, sharp, one, without fail in this room at eleven-thirty to-night.'

'Very good, sir.'

'Have you any idea where young Tuppy sleeps?'

'I could ascertain, sir.'

'Do so, Jeeves.'

In a few minutes he was back with the necessary informash.

'Mr Glossop is established in the Moat Room, sir.'

'Where's that?'

'The second door on the floor below this, sir.'

'Right ho, Jeeves. Are the studs in my shirt?'

'Yes, sir.'

'And the links also?'

'Yes, sir.'

'Then push me into it.'

The more I thought about this enterprise which a sense of duty and good citizenship had thrust upon me, the better it seemed to me. I am not a vindictive man, but I felt, as anybody would have felt in my place, that if fellows like young Tuppy are allowed to get away with it the whole fabric of Society and Civilization must inevitably crumble. The task to which I had set myself was one that involved hardship and discomfort, for it meant sitting up till well into the small hours and then padding down a cold corridor, but I did not shrink from it. After all, there is a lot to be said for family tradition. We Woosters did our bit in the Crusades.

It being Christmas Eve, there was, as I had foreseen, a good deal of revelry and what not. First, the village choir surged round and sang carols outside the front door, and then somebody suggested a dance, and after that we hung around chatting of this and that, so that it wasn't till past one that I got to my room. Allowing for everything, it didn't seem that it was going to be safe to start my little expedition till half-past two at the earliest: and I'm bound to say that it was only the utmost resolution that kept me from snuggling into the sheets and calling it a day. I'm not much of a lad now for late hours.

However, by half-past two everything appeared to be quiet. I shook off the mists of sleep, grabbed the good old stick-and-needle and off along the corridor. And presently, pausing outside the Moat Room, I turned the handle, found the door wasn't locked, and went in.

I suppose a burglar – I mean a real professional who works at the job six nights a week all the year round –

gets so that finding himself standing in the dark in somebody else's bedroom means absolutely nothing to him. But for a bird like me, who has had no previous experience, there's a lot to be said in favour of washing the whole thing out and closing the door gently and popping back to bed again. It was only by summoning up all the old bulldog courage of the Woosters, and reminding myself that, if I let this opportunity slip another might never occur, that I managed to stick out what you might call the initial minute of the binge. Then the weakness passed, and Bertram was himself again.

At first when I beetled in, the room had seemed as black as a coal-cellar: but after a bit things began to lighten. The curtains weren't quite drawn over the window and I could see a trifle of the scenery here and there. The bed was opposite the window, with the head against the wall and the end where the feet were jutting out towards where I stood, thus rendering it possible after one had sown the seed, so to speak, to make a quick getaway. There only remained now the rather tricky problem of locating the old hot-water bottle. I mean to say, the one thing you can't do if you want to carry a job like this through with secrecy and dispatch is to stand at the end of a fellow's bed, jabbing the blankets at random with a darning-needle. Before proceeding to anything in the nature of definite steps, it is imperative that you locate the bot.

I was a good deal cheered at this juncture to hear a fruity snore from the direction of the pillows. Reason told me that a bloke who could snore like that wasn't going to be awakened by a trifle. I edged forward and ran a hand in a gingerly sort of way over the coverlet. A moment later I had found the bulge. I steered the good old darning-needle on to it, gripped the stick, and shoved. Then, pulling out the weapon, I sidled towards the door, and in another moment would have been outside, buzzing for home and the good night's rest, when suddenly there was a crash that sent my spine shooting up through the top of my head and the contents of the bed sat up like a jack-in-the-box and said:

'Who's that?'

It just shows how your most careful strategic moves can be the very ones that dish your campaign. In order to facilitate the orderly retreat according to plan I had left the door open, and the beastly thing had slammed like a bomb.

But I wasn't giving much thought to the causes of the explosion, having other things to occupy my mind. What was disturbing me was the discovery that, whoever else the bloke in the bed might be, he was not young Tuppy. Tuppy has one of those high, squeaky voices that sound like the tenor of the village choir failing to hit a high note. This one was something in between the last Trump and a tiger calling for breakfast after being on a diet for a day or two. It was the sort of nasty, rasping voice you hear shouting "Fore!" when you're one of a slow foursome on the links and are holding up a couple of retired colonels. Among the qualities it lacked were kindliness, suavity and that sort of dove-like cooing note which makes a fellow feel he has found a friend.

I did not linger. Getting swiftly off the mark, I dived for the door-handle and was off and away, banging the door behind me. I may be a chump in many ways, as my Aunt Agatha will freely attest, but I know when and when not to be among those present.

And I was just about to do the stretch of corridor leading to the stairs in a split second under the record time for the course, when something brought me up with a sudden jerk. One moment, I was all dash and fire and speed; the next, an irresistible force had checked me in my stride and was holding me straining at the leash, as it were.

You know, sometimes it seems to me as if Fate were going out of its way to such an extent to snooter you that you wonder if it's worth while continuing to struggle. The night being a trifle chillier than the dickens, I had donned for this expedition a dressing-gown. It was the tail of this infernal garment that had caught in the door and pipped me at the eleventh hour.

The next moment the door had opened, light was streaming through it, and the bloke with the voice had grabbed me by the arm.

It was Sir Roderick Glossop.

The next thing that happened was a bit of a lull in the proceedings. For about three and a quarter seconds or possibly more we just stood there, drinking each other in, so to speak, the old boy still attached with a limpet-like grip to my elbow. If I hadn't been in a dressing-gown and he in pink pyjamas with a blue stripe, and if he hadn't been glaring quite so much as if he were shortly going to commit a murder, the tableau would have looked rather like one of those advertisements you see in the magazines, where the experienced elder is patting the young man's arm, and saying to him, "My boy, if you subscribe to the Mutt-Jeff Correspondence School of Oswego, Kan., as I did, you may some day, like me, become Third Assistant Vice-President of the Schenectady Consolidated Nail-File and Eyebrow Tweezer Corporation".

'You!' said Sir Roderick finally. And in this connection I want to state that it's all rot to say you can't hiss a word that hasn't an "s" in it. The way he pushed out that "You!" sounded like an angry cobra, and I am betraying no secrets when I mention that it did me no good whatsoever.

By rights, I suppose, at this point I ought to have said something. The best I could manage, however, was a faint, soft bleating sound. Even on ordinary social occasions, when meeting this bloke as man to man and with a clear conscience, I could never be completely at my ease: and now those eyebrows seemed to pierce me like a knife.

'Come in here,' he said, lugging me into the room. 'We don't want to wake the whole house. Now', he said, depositing me on the carpet and closing the door and doing a bit of eyebrow work, 'kindly inform me what is this latest manifestation of insanity?'

It seemed to me that a light and cheery laugh might help the thing along. So I had a pop at one.

'Don't gibber!' said my genial host. And I'm bound to admit that the light and cheery hadn't come out quite as I'd intended.

I pulled myself together with a strong effort.

'Awfully sorry about all this,' I said in a hearty sort of voice. 'The fact is, I thought you were Tuppy.'

'Kindly refrain from inflicting your idiotic slang on me. What do you mean by the adjective "tuppy"?'

'It isn't so much an adjective, don't you know. More of a noun, I should think, if you examine it squarely. What I mean to say is, I thought you were your nephew.'

'You thought I was my nephew? Why should I be my nephew?'

'What I'm driving at is, I thought this was his room.'

'My nephew and I changed rooms. I have a great dislike for sleeping on an upper floor. I am nervous about fire.'

For the first time since this interview had started, I braced up a trifle. The injustice of the whole thing stirred me to such an extent that for a moment I lost that sense of being a toad under the harrow which had been cramping my style up till now. I even went so far as to eye this pink-pyjamed poltroon with a good deal of contempt and loathing. Just because he had this craven fear of fire and this selfish preference for letting Tuppy be cooked instead of himself should the emergency occur, my nicely-reasoned plans had gone up the spout. I gave him a look, and I think I may even have snorted a bit.

'I should have thought that your man-servant would have informed you,' said Sir Roderick, 'that we contemplated making this change. I met him shortly before luncheon and told him to tell you.'

I reeled. Yes, it is not too much to say that I reeled. This extraordinary statement had taken me amidships without any preparation, and it staggered me. That Jeeves had been aware all along that this old crumb would be the occupant of the bed which I was proposing to prod with darning-needles and had let me rush upon my doom without a word of warning was almost beyond belief. You might say I was aghast. Yes, practically aghast.

'You told Jeeves that you were going to sleep in this room?' I gasped.

'I did. I was aware that you and my nephew were on terms of intimacy, and I wished to spare myself the possibility of a visit from you. I confess that it never occurred to me that such a visit was to be anticipated at three o'clock in the morning. What the devil do you mean,' he barked, suddenly hotting up, 'by prowling about the house at this hour? And what is that thing in your hand?'

I looked down, and found that I was still grasping the stick. I give you my honest word that, what with the maelstrom of emotions into which his revelation about Jeeves had cast me, the discovery came as an absolute surprise.

'This?' I said. 'Oh, yes.'

'What do you mean, Oh yes? What is it?'

'Well, it's a long story – '

'We have the night before us.'

'It's this way. I will ask you to picture me some weeks ago, perfectly peaceful and inoffensive, after dinner at the Drones, smoking a thoughtful cigarette and – '

I broke off. The man wasn't listening. He was goggling in a rapt sort of way at the end of the bed, from which there had now begun to drip on to the carpet a series of drops.

'Good heavens!'

'– thoughtful cigarette and chatting pleasantly of this and that – '

I broke off again. He had lifted the sheets and was gazing at the corpse of the hot-water bottle.

'Did you do this?' he said in a low, strangled sort of voice.

'Er – yes. As a matter of fact, yes. I was just going to tell you – '

'And your aunt tried to persuade me that you were not insane!'

'I'm not. Absolutely not. If you'll just let me explain.'

'I will do nothing of the kind.'

'It all began – '

'Silence!'

'Right-ho.'

He did some deep-breathing exercises through the nose.

'My bed is drenched!'

'The way it all began –'

'Be quiet!' He heaved somewhat for awhile. 'You wretched, miserable idiot,' he said, 'kindly inform me which bedroom you are supposed to be occupying?'

'It's on the floor above. The Clock Room.'

'Thank you. I will find it.'

'Eh?'

He gave me the eyebrow.

'I propose' he said, 'to pass the remainder of the night in your room, where, I presume, there is a bed in a condition to be slept in. You may bestow yourself as comfortably as you can here. I will wish you good-night.'

He buzzed off, leaving me flat.

Well, we Woosters are old campaigners. We can take the rough with the smooth. But to say that I liked the prospect now before me would be paltering with the truth. One glance at the bed told me that any idea of sleeping there was out. A goldfish could have done it, but not Bertram. After a bit of a look round, I decided that the best chance of getting a sort of night's rest was to doss as well as I could in the arm-chair. I pinched a couple of pillows off the bed, shoved the hearth-rug over my knees, and sat down and started counting sheep.

But it wasn't any good. The old lemon was sizzling much too much to admit of anything in the nature of slumber. This hideous revelation of the blackness of Jeeves's treachery kept coming back to me every time I nearly succeeded in dropping off: and, what's more, it seemed to get colder and colder as the long night wore on. I was just wondering if I would ever get to sleep again in this world when a voice at my elbow said 'Good-morning, sir' and I sat up with a jerk.

I could have sworn I hadn't so much as dozed off for even a minute, but apparently I had. For the curtains were drawn back and daylight was coming in through the window and there was Jeeves standing beside me with a cup of tea on a tray.

'Merry Christmas, sir!'

I reached out a feeble hand for the restoring brew. I swallowed a mouthful or two, and felt a little better. I was aching in every limb and the dome felt like lead, but I was now able to think with a certain amount of clearness, and I fixed the man with a stony eye and prepared to let him have it.

'You think so, do you?' I said. 'Much, let me tell you, depends on what you mean by the adjective "merry". If, moreover, you suppose that it is going to be merry for you, correct that impression, Jeeves,' I said, taking another half-oz., of tea and speaking in a cold, measured voice, 'I wish to ask you one question. Did you or did you not know that Sir Roderick Glossop was sleeping in this room last night?'

'Yes, sir.'

'You admit it!'

'Yes, sir.'

'And you didn't tell me!'

'No, sir. I thought it would be more judicious not to do so.'

'Jeeves –'

'If you will allow me to explain, sir.'

'Explain!'

'I was aware that my silence might lead to something in the nature of an embarrassing contretemps, sir – '

'You thought that, did you?'

'Yes, sir.'

'You were a good guesser,' I said, sucking down further Bohea.

'But it seemed to me, sir, that whatever might occur was all for the best.'

I would have put in a crisp word or two here, but he carried on without giving me the opp.

'I thought that possibly, on reflection, sir, your views being what they are, you would prefer your relations with Sir Roderick Glossop and his family to be distant rather than cordial.'

'My views? What do you mean, my views?'

'As regards a matrimonial alliance with Miss Honoria Glossop, sir.'

Something like an electric shock seemed to zip through me. The man had opened up a new line of thought. I suddenly saw what he was driving at, and realized all in a flash that I had been wronging this faithful fellow. All the while I supposed he had been landing me in the soup, he had really been steering me away from it. It was like those stories one used to read as a kid about the traveller going along on a dark night and his dog grabs him by the leg of his trousers and he says "Down, sir! What are you doing, Rover?" and the dog hangs on and he gets rather hot under the collar and curses a bit but the dog won't let him go and then suddenly the moon shines through the clouds and he finds he's been standing on the edge of a precipice and one more step would have – well, anyway, you get the idea: and what I'm driving at is that much the same sort of thing seemed to have been happening now.

It's perfectly amazing how a fellow will let himself get off his guard and ignore the perils which surround him. I give you my honest word, it had never struck me till this morning that my Aunt Agatha had been scheming to get me in right with Sir Roderick so that I should eventually be received back into the fold, if you see what I mean, and subsequently pushed off on Honoria.

'My God, Jeeves!' I said, paling.

'Precisely, sir.'

'You think there was a risk?'

'I do, sir. A very grave risk.'

A disturbing thought struck me.

'But, Jeeves, on calm reflection won't Sir Roderick have gathered by now that my objective was young Tuppy and that puncturing his hot-water bottle was just one of those things that occur when the Yule-tide spirit is abroad – one of those things that have to be overlooked and taken with the indulgent smile and the fatherly shake of the head? I mean to say, Young Blood and all that sort of thing? What I mean is he'll realize that I wasn't trying to snooter him, and then all the good work will have been wasted.'

'No, sir. I fancy not. That might possibly have been Sir Roderick's mental reaction, had it not been for the second incident.'

'The second incident?'

'During the night, sir, while Sir Roderick was occupying your bed, somebody entered the room, pierced his hot-water bottle with some sharp instrument, and vanished in the darkness.'

I could make nothing of this.

'What! Do you think I walked in my sleep?'

'No, sir. It was young Mr Glossop who did it. I encountered him this morning, sir, shortly before I came here. He was in cheerful spirits and enquired of me how you were feeling about the incident. Not being aware that his victim had been Sir Roderick.'

'But, Jeeves, what an amazing coincidence!'

'Sir?'

'Why, young Tuppy getting exactly the same idea as I did. Or, rather, as Miss Wickham did. You can't say that's not rummy. A miracle, I call it.'

'Not altogether, sir. It appears that he received the suggestion from the young lady.'

'From Miss Wickham?'

'Yes, sir.'

'You mean to say that, after she had put me up to the scheme of puncturing Tuppy's hot-water bottle, she went away and tipped Tuppy off to puncturing mine?'

'Precisely, sir. She is a young lady with a keen sense of humour, sir.'

I sat there, you might say stunned. When I thought how near I had come to offering the heart and hand to a girl capable of double-crossing a strong man's honest love like that, I shivered.

'Are you cold, sir?'

'No, Jeeves. Just shuddering.'

'The occurrence, if I may take the liberty of saying so, sir, will perhaps lend colour to the view which I put forward yesterday that Miss Wickham, though in many respects a charming young lady – '

I raised a hand.

'Say no more, Jeeves,' I replied. 'Love is dead.'

'Very good, sir.'

I brooded for a while.

'You've seen Sir Roderick this morning, then?'

'Yes, sir.'

'How did he seem?'

'A trifle feverish, sir.'

'Feverish?'

'A little emotional, sir. He expressed a strong desire to meet you, sir.'

'What would you advise?'

'If you were to slip out by the back entrance as soon as you are dressed, sir, it would be possible for you to make your way across the field without being observed and reach the village, where you could hire an auto-

mobile to take you to London. I could bring on your
effects later in your own car.'

'But London, Jeeves? Is any man safe? My Aunt
Agatha is in London.'

'Yes, sir.'

'Well, then?'

He regarded me for a moment with a fathomless eye.
'I think the best plan, sir, would be for you to leave
England, which is not pleasant at this time of the year,
for some little while. I would not take the liberty of
dictating your movements, sir, but as you already have
accommodation engaged on the Blue Train for Monte
Carlo for the day after to-morrow – '

'But you cancelled the booking?'

'No, sir.'

'I thought you had.'

'No, sir.'

'I told you to.'

'Yes, sir. It was remiss of me, but the matter slipped
my mind.'

'Oh?'

'Yes, sir.'

'All right, Jeeves. Monte Carlo ho, then.'

'Very good, sir.'

'It's lucky, as things have turned out, that you forgot
to cancel that booking.'

'Very fortunate indeed, sir. If you will wait here, sir,
I will return to your room and procure a suit of clothes.'

=7=
JEEVES AND THE SONG OF SONGS

Another day had dawned all hot and fresh and, in pursuance of my unswerving policy at that time, I was singing "Sonny Boy" in my bath, when there was a soft step without and Jeeves's voice came filtering through the woodwork.

'I beg your pardon, sir.'

I had just got to that bit about the Angels being lonely, where you need every ounce of concentration in order to make the spectacular finish, but I signed off courteously.

'Yes, Jeeves? Say on.'

'Mr Glossop, sir.'

'What about him?'

'He is in the sitting-room, sir.'

'Young Tuppy Glossop?'

'Yes, sir.'

'In the sitting-room?'

'Yes, sir.'

'Desiring speech with me?'

'Yes, sir.'

'H'm!'

'Sir?'

'I only said H'm.'

And I'll tell you why I said H'm. It was because the man's story had interested me strangely. The news that

Tuppy was visiting me at my flat, at an hour when he must have known that I would be in my bath and consequently in a strong strategic position to heave a wet sponge at him, surprised me considerably.

I hopped out with some briskness and, slipping a couple of towels about the limbs and torso, made for the sitting-room. I found young Tuppy at the piano, playing "Sonny Boy" with one finger.

'What ho!' I said, not without a certain hauteur.

'Oh, hullo, Bertie,' said young Tuppy. 'I say, Bertie, I want to see you about something important.'

It seemed to me that the bloke was embarrassed. He had moved to the mantelpiece, and now he broke a vase in rather a constrained way.

'The fact is, Bertie, I'm engaged.'

'Engaged?'

'Engaged,' said young Tuppy, coyly dropping a photograph frame into the fender. 'Practically, that is.'

'Practically?'

'Yes. You'll like her, Bertie. Her name is Cora Bellinger. She's studying for Opera. Wonderful voice she has. Also dark, flashing eyes and a great soul.'

'How do you mean, practically?'

'Well, it's this way. Before ordering the trousseau, there is one little point she wants cleared up. You see, what with her great soul and all that, she has a rather serious outlook on life: and the one thing she absolutely bars is anything in the shape of hearty humour. You know, practical joking and so forth. She said if she thought I was a practical joker she would never speak to me again. And unfortunately she appears to have heard about that little affair at the Drones – I expect you have forgotten all about that, Bertie?'

'I have not!'

'No, no, not forgotten exactly. What I mean is,

nobody laughs more heartily at the recollection than you. And what I want you to do, old man, is to seize an early opportunity of taking Cora aside and categorically denying that there is any truth in the story. My happiness, Bertie, is in your hands, if you know what I mean.'

Well, of course, if he put it like that, what could I do? We Woosters have our code.

'Oh, all right,' I said, but far from brightly.

'Splendid fellow!'

'When do I meet this blighted female?'

'Don't call her "this blighted female", Bertie, old man. I have planned all that out. I will bring her round here to-day for a spot of lunch.'

'What!'

'At one-thirty. Right. Good. Fine. Thanks. I knew I could rely on you.'

He pushed off, and I turned to Jeeves, who had shimmered in with the morning meal.

'Lunch for three to-day, Jeeves,' I said.

'Very good, sir.'

'You know, Jeeves, it's a bit thick. You remember my telling you about what Mr Glossop did to me that night at the Drones?'

'Yes, sir.'

'For months I have been cherishing dreams of getting a bit of my own back. And now, so far from crushing him into the dust, I've got to fill him and fiancée with rich food and generally rally round and be the good angel.'

'Life is like that, sir.'

'True, Jeeves. What have we here?' I asked, inspecting the tray.

'Kippered herrings, sir.'

'And I shouldn't wonder,' I said, for I was in thought-

91

ful mood, 'if even herrings haven't troubles of their own.'

'Quite possibly, sir.'

'I mean, apart from getting kippered.'

'Yes, sir.'

'And so it goes on, Jeeves, so it goes on.'

I can't say I exactly saw eye to eye with young Tuppy in his admiration for the Bellinger female. Delivered on the mat at one-twenty-five, she proved to be an upstanding light-heavyweight of some thirty summers, with a commanding eye and a square chin which I, personally, would have steered clear of. She seemed to me a good deal like what Cleopatra would have been after going in too freely for the starches and cereals. I don't know why it is, but women who have anything to do with Opera, even if they're only studying for it, always appear to run to surplus poundage.

Tuppy, however, was obviously all for her. His whole demeanour, both before and during lunch, was that of one striving to be worthy of a noble soul. When Jeeves offered him a cocktail, he practically recoiled as from a serpent. It was terrible to see the change which love had effected in the man. The spectacle put me off my food.

At half-past two, the Bellinger left to go to a singing lesson. Tuppy trotted after her to the door, bleating and frisking a goodish bit, and then came back and looked at me in a goofy sort of way.

'Well, Bertie?'

'Well, what?'

'I mean, isn't she?'

'Oh, rather,' I said, humouring the poor fish.

'Wonderful eyes?'

'Oh, rather.'

'Wonderful figure?'

'Oh, quite.'

'Wonderful voice?'

Here I was able to intone the response with a little more heartiness. The Bellinger, at Tuppy's request, had sung us a few songs before digging in at the trough, and nobody could have denied that her pipes were in great shape. Plaster was still falling from the ceiling.

'Terrific,' I said.

Tuppy sighed, and, having helped himself to about four inches of whisky and one of soda, took a deep, refreshing draught.

'Ah!' he said. 'I needed that.'

'Why didn't you have it at lunch?'

'Well, it's this way,' said Tuppy. 'I have not actually ascertained what Cora's opinions are on the subject of taking of slight snorts from time to time, but I thought it more prudent to lay off. The view I took was that laying off would seem to indicate the serious mind. It is touch-and-go, as you might say, at the moment, and the smallest thing may turn the scale.'

'What beats me is how on earth you expect to make her think you've got a mind at all – let alone a serious one.'

'I have my methods.'

'I bet they're rotten.'

'You do, do you?' said Tuppy warmly. 'Well, let me tell you, my lad, that that's exactly what they're anything but. I am handling this affair with consummate generalship. Do you remember Beefy Bingham who was at Oxford with us?'

'I ran into him only the other day. He's a parson now.'

'Yes. Down in the East End. Well, he runs a Lads' Club for the local toughs – you know the sort of thing

– cocoa and backgammon in the reading-room and
occasional clean, bright entertainments in the Oddfellows' Hall: and I've been helping him. I don't suppose
I've passed an evening away from the backgammon
board for weeks. Cora is extremely pleased. I've got her
to promise to sing on Tuesday at Beefy's next clean,
bright entertainment.'

'You have?'

'I absolutely have. And now mark my devilish ingen-
uity, Bertie. I'm going to sing, too.'

'Why do you suppose that's going to get you
anywhere?'

'Because the way I intend to sing the song I intend
to sing will prove to her that there are great deeps in
my nature, whose existence she has not suspected. She
will see that rough, unlettered audience wiping the tears
out of its bally eyes and she will say to herself "What
ho! The old egg really has a soul!" For it is not one of
your mouldy comic songs, Bertie. No low buffoonery
of that sort for me. It is all about Angela being lonely
and what not – '

I uttered a sharp cry.

'You don't mean you're going to sing "Sonny Boy"?'

'I jolly well do.'

I was shocked. Yes, dash it, I was shocked. You see,
I held strong views on "Sonny Boy". I considered it a
song only to be attempted by a few of the elect in the
privacy of the bathroom. And the thought of it being
murdered in open Oddfellows' Hall by a man who
could treat a pal as young Tuppy had treated me that
night at the Drones sickened me. Yes, sickened me.

I hadn't time, however, to express my horror and
disgust, for at this juncture Jeeves came in.

'Mrs Travers has just rung up on the telephone, sir.

She desired me to say that she will be calling to see you in a few minutes.'

'Contents noted, Jeeves,' I said. 'Now listen, Tuppy – '

I stopped. The fellow wasn't there.

'What have you done with him, Jeeves?' I asked.

'Mr Glossop has left, sir.'

'Left? How can he have left? He was sitting there – '

'That is the front door closing now, sir.'

'But what made him shoot off like that?'

'Possibly Mr Glossop did not wish to meet Mrs Travers, sir.'

'Why not?'

'I could not say, sir. But undoubtedly at the mention of Mrs Travers' name he rose very swiftly.'

'Strange, Jeeves.'

'Yes, sir.'

I turned to a subject of more moment.

'Jeeves,' I said. 'Mr Glossop proposes to sing "Sonny Boy" at an entertainment down in the East End next Tuesday.'

'Indeed, sir?'

'Before an audience consisting mainly of coster-mongers, with a sprinkling of whelk-stall owners, purveyors of blood-oranges, and minor pugilists.'

'Indeed, sir?'

'Make a note to remind me to be there. He will infallibly get the bird, and I want to witness his downfall.'

'Very good, sir.'

'And when Mrs Travers arrives, I shall be in the sitting-room.'

Those who know Bertram Wooster best are aware that in his journey through life he is impeded and generally snootered by about as scaly a platoon of aunts as was ever assembled. But there is one exception to the general ghastliness – viz., my Aunt Dahlia. She married old Tom Travers the year Blue-bottle won the Cambridge-shire, and is one of the best. It is always a pleasure to me to chat with her, and it was with a courtly geniality that I rose to receive her as she sailed over the threshold at about two fifty-five.

She seemed somewhat perturbed, and snapped into the agenda without delay. Aunt Dahlia is one of those big, hearty women. She used to go in a lot for hunting, and she generally speaks as if she had just sighted a fox on a hillside half a mile away.

'Bertie,' she cried, in a manner of one encouraging a bevy of hounds to renewed efforts. 'I want your help.'

'And you shall have it, Aunt Dahlia,' I replied suavely. 'I can honestly say that there is no one to whom I would more readily do a good turn than yourself; no one to whom I am more delighted to be – '

'Less of it,' she begged, 'less of it. You know that friend of yours, young Glossop?'

'He's just been lunching here.'

'He has, has he? Well, I wish you'd poisoned his soup.'

'We didn't have soup. And, when you describe him as a friend of mine, I wouldn't quite say the term absol-utely squared with the facts. Some time ago, one night when we had been dining together at the Drones – '

At this point Aunt Dahlia – a little brusquely, it seemed to me – said that she would rather wait for the story of my life till she could get it in book-form. I could see now that she was definitely not her usual sunny self, so I shelved my personal grievances and asked what was biting her.

'It's that young hound Glossop,' she said.

'What's he been doing?'

'Breaking Angela's heart.' (Angela. Daughter of above. My cousin. Quite a good egg.)

'Breaking Angela's heart?'

'Yes . . . Breaking . . . Angela's HEART!'

'You say he's breaking Angela's heart?'

She begged me in rather a feverish way to suspend the vaudeville cross-talk stuff.

'How's he doing that?' I asked.

'With his neglect. With his low, callous, double-crossing duplicity.'

'Duplicity is the word, Aunt Dahlia,' I said. 'In treating of young Tuppy Glossop, it springs naturally to the lips. Let me just tell you what he did to me one night at the Drones. We had finished dinner – '

'Ever since the beginning of the season, up till about three weeks ago, he was all over Angela. The sort of thing which, when I was a girl, we should have described as courting – '

'Or wooing?'

'Wooing or courting, whichever you like.'

'Whichever *you* like, Aunt Dahlia,' I said courteously.

'Well, anyway, he haunted the house, lapped up daily lunches, danced with her half the night, and so on, till naturally the poor kid, who's quite off her oats about him, took it for granted that it was only a question of time before he suggested that they should feed for life out of the same crib. And now he's gone and dropped her like a hot brick, and I hear he's infatuated with some girl he met at a Chelsea tea-party – a girl named – now, what was it?'

'Cora Bellinger.'

'How do you know?'

'She was lunching here to-day.'

'He brought her?'

'Yes.'

'What's she like?'

'Pretty massive. In shape, a bit on the lines of the Albert Hall.'

'Did he seem very fond of her?'

'Couldn't take his eyes off the chassis.'

'The modern young man,' said Aunt Dahlia, 'is a congenital idiot and wants a nurse to lead him by the hand and some strong attendant to kick him regularly at intervals of a quarter of an hour.'

I tried to point out the silver lining.

'If you ask me, Aunt Dahlia,' I said, 'I think Angela is well out of it. This Glossop is a tough baby. One of London's toughest. I was trying to tell you just now what he did to me one night at the Drones. First having got me in a sporting mood with a bottle of the ripest, he betted I wouldn't swing myself across the swimming-bath by the ropes and rings. I knew I could do it on my head, so I took him on, exulting in the fun, so to speak. And when I'd done half the trip and was going as strong as dammit, I found he had looped the last rope back against the rail, leaving me no alternative but to drop into the depths and swim ashore in correct evening costume.'

'He did?'

'He certainly did. It was months ago, and I haven't got really dry yet. You wouldn't want your daughter to marry a man capable of a thing like that?'

'On the contrary, you restore my faith in the young hound. I see that there must be lots of good in him, after all. And I want this Bellinger business broken up, Bertie.'

'How?'

'I don't care how. Any way you please.'

'But what can I do?'

'Do? Why, put the whole thing before your man Jeeves. Jeeves will find a way. One of the most capable fellers I ever met. Put the thing squarely up to Jeeves and tell him to let his mind play round the topic.'

'There may be something in what you say, Aunt Dahlia,' I said thoughtfully.

'Of course there is,' said Aunt Dahlia. 'A little thing like this will be child's play to Jeeves. Get him working on it, and I'll look in to-morrow to hear the result.'

With which, she biffed off, and I summoned Jeeves to the presence.

'Jeeves,' I said, 'you have heard all?'

'Yes, sir.'

'I thought you would. My Aunt Dahlia has what you might call a carrying voice. Has it ever occurred to you that, if all other sources of income failed, she could make a good living calling the cattle home across the Sands of Dee?'

'I had not considered the point, sir, but no doubt you are right.'

'Well, how do we go? What is your reaction? I think we should do our best to help and assist.'

'Yes, sir.'

'I am fond of my Aunt Dahlia and I am fond of my cousin Angela. Fond of them both, if you get my drift. What the misguided girl finds to attract her in young Tuppy, I cannot say, Jeeves, and you cannot say. But apparently she loves the man – which shows it can be done, a thing I wouldn't have believed myself – and is pining away like – '

'Patience on a monument, sir.'

'Like Patience, as you very shrewdly remark, on a monument. So we must cluster round. Bend your brain to the problem, Jeeves. It is one that will tax you to the uttermost.'

Aunt Dahlia blew in on the morrow, and I rang the bell for Jeeves. He appeared looking brainier than one could have believed possible – sheer intellect shining from every feature – and I could see at once that the engine had been turning over.

'Speak, Jeeves,' I said.

'Very good, sir.'

'You have brooded?'

'Yes, sir.'

'With what success?'

'I have a plan, sir, which I fancy may produce satisfactory results.'

'Let's have it,' said Aunt Dahlia.

'In affairs of this description, madam, the first essential is to study the psychology of the individual.'

'The what of the individual?'

'The psychology, madam.'

'He means the psychology,' I said. 'And by psychology, Jeeves, you imply – ?'

'The natures and dispositions of the principals in the matter, sir.'

'You mean, what they're like?'

'Precisely, sir.'

'Does he talk like this to you when you're alone, Bertie?' asked Aunt Dahlia.

'Sometimes. Occasionally. And, on the other hand, sometimes not. Proceed, Jeeves.'

'Well, sir, if I may say so, the thing that struck me most forcibly about Miss Bellinger when she was under my observation was that hers was a somewhat hard and intolerant nature. I could envisage Miss Bellinger applauding success. I could not so easily see her pitying and sympathizing with failure. Possibly you will recall, sir, her attitude when Mr Glossop endeavoured to light her cigarette with his automatic lighter? I thought I detected a certain impatience at his inability to produce the necessary flame.'

'True, Jeeves. She ticked him off.'

'Precisely, sir.'

'Let me get this straight,' said Aunt Dahlia, looking a bit fogged. 'You think that, if he goes on trying to light her cigarettes with his automatic lighter long enough, she will eventually get fed up and hand him the mitten? Is that the idea?'

'I merely mentioned the episode, madam, as an indication of Miss Bellinger's somewhat ruthless nature.'

'Ruthless,' I said, 'is right. The Bellinger is hard-boiled. Those eyes. That chin. I could read them. A woman of blood and iron, if ever there was one.'

'Precisely, sir. I think, therefore, that, should Miss Bellinger be a witness of Mr Glossop appearing to disadvantage in public, she would cease to entertain affection for him. In the event, for instance, of his failing to please the audience on Tuesday with his singing –'

I saw daylight.

'By Jove, Jeeves! You mean if he gets the bird, all will be off?'

'I shall be greatly surprised if such is not the case, sir.'

I shook my head.

'We cannot leave this thing to chance, Jeeves. Young Tuppy, singing "Sonny Boy," is the likeliest prospect for the bird that I can think of – but, no – you must see for yourself that we can't simply trust to luck.'

'We need not trust to luck, sir. I would suggest that you approach your friend, Mr Bingham, and volunteer your services as a performer at his forthcoming entertainment. It could readily be arranged that you sang immediately before Mr Glossop. I fancy, sir, that, if Mr Glossop were to sing "Sonny Boy" directly after you, too, had sung "Sonny Boy", the audience would respond satisfactorily. By the time, Mr Glossop began to sing, they would have lost their taste for that particular song and would express their feelings warmly.'

'Jeeves,' said Aunt Dahlia, 'you're a marvel!'

'Thank you, madam.'

'Jeeves,' I said, 'you're an ass!'

'What do you mean, he's an ass?' said Aunt Dahlia hotly. 'I think it's the greatest scheme I ever heard.'

'Me sing "Sonny Boy" at Beefy Bingham's clean, bright entertainment? I can see myself!'

'You sing it daily in your bath, sir. Mr Wooster,' said Jeeves, turning to Aunt Dahlia, 'has a pleasant, light baritone – '

'I bet he has,' said Aunt Dahlia.

I froze the man with a look.

'Between singing "Sonny Boy" in one's bath, Jeeves, and singing it before a hall full of assorted blood-orange merchants and their young, there is a substantial difference.'

'Bertie,' said Aunt Dahlia, 'you'll sing, and like it!'

'I will not.'

'Bertie!'

'Nothing will induce – '

'Bertie,' said Aunt Dahlia firmly, 'you will sing "Sonny Boy" on Tuesday, the third *prox.*, and sing it like a lark at sunrise or may an aunt's curse – '

'I won't'

'Think of Angela!'

'Dash Angela!'

'Bertie!'

'No, I mean, hang it all!'

'You won't?'

'No, I won't.'

'That is your last word, is it?'

'It is. Once and for all, Aunt Dahlia, nothing will induce me to let out so much as a single note.'

And so that afternoon I sent a pre-paid wire to Beefy Bingham, offering my services in the cause, and by nightfall the thing was fixed up. I was billed to perform next but one after the intermission. Following me, came Tuppy. And, immediately after him, Miss Cora Bellinger, the well-known operatic soprano.

'Jeeves,' I said that evening – and I said it coldly – 'I shall be obliged if you will pop round to the nearest music-shop and procure me a copy of "Sonny Boy". It will now be necessary for me to learn both verse and refrain. Of the trouble and nervous strain which this will involve, I say nothing.'

'Very good, sir.'

'But this I do say – '

'I had better be starting immediately, sir, or the shop will be closed.'

'Ha!' I said.

And I meant it to sting.

Although I had steeled myself to the ordeal before me and had set out full of the calm, quiet courage which makes men do desperate deeds with careless smiles, I must admit that there was a moment, just after I had entered the Oddfellows' Hall at Bermondsey East and run an eye over the assembled pleasure-seekers, when it needed all the bull-dog pluck of the Woosters to keep me from calling it a day and taking a cab back to civilization. The clean, bright entertainment was in full swing when I arrived, and somebody who looked as if he might be the local undertaker was reciting "Gunga Din". And the audience, though not actually chi-yiking in the full technical sense of the term, had a grim look which I didn't like at all. The mere sight of them gave me the sort of feeling Shadrach, Meshach and Abednego must have had when preparing to enter the burning, fiery furnace.

Scanning the multitude, it seemed to me that they were for the nonce suspending judgment. Did you ever tap on the door of one of those New York speakeasy places and see the grille snap back and a Face appear? There is one long, silent moment when its eyes are fixed on yours and all your past life seems to rise up before you. Then you say that you are a friend of Mr Zinzinheimer and he told you they would treat you right if you mentioned his name, and the strain relaxes. Well, these costermongers and whelkstallers appeared to me to be looking just like that Face. Start something, they seemed to say, and they would know what to do about it. And I couldn't help feeling that my singing "Sonny Boy" would come, in their opinion, under the head of starting something.

'A nice, full house, sir,' said a voice at my elbow. It was Jeeves, watching the proceedings with an indulgent eye.

'You here, Jeeves?' I said, coldly.

'Yes, sir. I have been present since the commencement.'

'Oh?' I said. 'Any casualties yet?'

'Sir?'

'You know what I mean, Jeeves,' I said sternly, 'and don't pretend you don't. Anybody got the bird yet?'

'Oh, no, sir.'

'I shall be the first, you think?'

'No, sir. I see no reason to expect such a misfortune. I anticipate that you will be well received.'

A sudden thought struck me.

'And you think everything will go according to plan?'

'Yes, sir.'

'Well, I don't,' I said. 'And I'll tell you why I don't. I've spotted a flaw in your beastly scheme.'

'A flaw, sir?'

'Yes. Do you suppose for a moment that, if when Mr Glossop hears me singing that dashed song, he'll come calmly on a minute after me and sing it too? Use your intelligence, Jeeves. He will perceive the chasm in his path and pause in time. He will back out and refuse to go on at all.'

'Mr Glossop will not hear you sing, sir. At my advice, he has stepped across the road to the Jug and Bottle, an establishment immediately opposite the hall, and he intends to remain there until it is time for him to appear on the platform.'

'Oh?' I said.

'If I might suggest it, sir, there is another house named the Goat and Grapes only a short distance down the street. I think it might be a judicious move – '

'If I were to put a bit of custom in their way?'

'It would ease the nervous strain of waiting, sir.'

I had not been feeling any too pleased with the man for having let me in for this ghastly binge, but at these words, I'm bound to say, my austerity softened a trifle. He was undoubtedly right. He had studied the psychology of the individual, and it had not led him astray. A quiet ten minutes at the Goat and Grapes was exactly what my system required. To buzz off there and inhale a couple of swift whisky-and-sodas was with Bertram Wooster the work of a moment.

The treatment worked like magic. What they had put into the stuff, besides vitriol, I could not have said; but it completely altered my outlook on life. That curious, gulpy feeling passed. I was no longer conscious of the sagging sensation at the knees. The limbs ceased to quiver gently, the tongue became loosened in its socket, and the backbone stiffened. Pausing merely to order and swallow another of the same, I bade the barmaid a cheery good night, nodded affably to one or two fellows in the bar whose faces I liked, and came prancing back to the hall, ready for anything.

And shortly afterwards I was on the platform with about a million bulging eyes goggling up at me. There was a rummy sort of buzzing in my ears, and then through the buzzing I heard the sound of a piano starting to tinkle: and, commending my soul to God, I took a good, long breath and charged in.

Well, it was a close thing. The whole incident is a bit blurred, but I seem to recollect a kind of murmur as I hit the refrain. I thought at the time it was an attempt on the part of the many-headed to join in the chorus, and at the moment it rather encouraged me. I passed the thing over the larynx with all the vim at my disposal, hit the high note, and off gracefully into the wings. I didn't come on again to take a bow. I just receded and oiled round to where Jeeves awaited me among the standees at the back.

'Well, Jeeves,' I said, anchoring myself at his side and brushing the honest sweat from the brow, 'they didn't rush the platform.'

'No, sir.'

'But you can spread it about that that's the last time I perform outside my bath. My swan-song, Jeeves. Anybody who wants to hear me in future must present himself at the bathroom door and shove his ear against the keyhole. I may be wrong, but it seemed to me that towards the end they were hotting up a trifle. The bird was hovering in the air. I could hear the beating of its wings.'

'I did detect a certain restlessness, sir, in the audience.

I fancy they had lost their taste for that particular melody.'

'Eh?'

'I should have informed you earlier, sir, that the song had already been sung twice before you arrived.'

'What!'

'Yes, sir. Once by a lady and once by a gentleman. It is a very popular song, sir.'

I gaped at the man. That, with this knowledge, he could calmly have allowed the young master to step straight into the jaws of death, so to speak, paralysed me. It seemed to show that the old feudal spirit had passed away altogether. I was about to give him my views on the matter in no uncertain fashion, when I was stopped by the spectacle of young Tuppy lurching on to the platform.

Young Tuppy had the unmistakable air of a man who has recently been round to the Jug and Bottle. A few cheery cries of welcome, presumably from some of his backgammon-playing pals who felt that blood was thicker than water, had the effect of causing the genial smile on his face to widen till it nearly met at the back. He was plainly feeling about as good as a man can feel and still remain on his feet. He waved a kindly hand to his supporters, and bowed in a regal sort of manner, rather like an Eastern monarch acknowledging the plaudits of the mob.

Then the female at the piano struck up the opening bars of "Sonny Boy", and Tuppy swelled like a balloon, clasped his hands together, rolled his eyes up at the ceiling in a manner denoting Soul, and began.

I think the populace was too stunned for the moment to take immediate steps. It may seem incredible, but I give you my word that young Tuppy got right through the verse without so much as a murmur. Then they all seemed to pull themselves together.

A costermonger, roused, is a terrible thing. I had never seen the proletariat really stirred before, and I'm bound to say it rather awed me. I mean, it gave you some idea of what it must have been like during the French Revolution. From every corner of the hall there proceeded simultaneously the sort of noise which you hear, they tell me, at one of those East End boxing places when the referee disqualifies the popular favourite and makes the quick dash for life. And then they passed beyond mere words and began to introduce the vegetable motive.

I don't know why, but somehow I had got it into my head that the first thing thrown at Tuppy would be a potato. One gets these fancies. It was, however, as a matter of fact, a banana, and I saw in an instant that the choice had been made by wiser heads than mine. These blokes who have grown up from childhood in the knowledge of how to treat a dramatic entertainment that doesn't please them are aware by a sort of instinct just what to do for the best, and the moment I saw the banana splash on Tuppy's shirt-front I realized how infinitely more effective and artistic it was than any potato could have been.

Not that the potato school of thought had not also its supporters. As the proceedings warmed up, I noticed several intelligent-looking fellows who threw nothing else.

The effect on young Tuppy was rather remarkable. His eyes bulged and his hair seemed to stand up, and yet his mouth went on opening and shutting, and you could see that in a dazed, automatic way he was still singing "Sonny Boy". Then, coming out of his trance, he began to pull for the shore with some rapidity. The last seen of him, he was beating a tomato to the exit by a short head.

Presently the tumult and the shouting died. I turned to Jeeves.

'Painful, Jeeves,' I said. 'But what would you?'

'Yes, sir.'

'The surgeon's knife, what?'

'Precisely, sir.'

'Well, with this happening beneath her eyes, I think we may definitely consider the Glossop-Bellinger romance off.'

'Yes, sir.'

At this point old Beefy Bingham came out on to the platform.

'Ladies and gentlemen,' said old Beefy.

I supposed that he was about to rebuke his flock for the recent expression of feeling. But such was not the case. No doubt he was accustomed by now to the wholesome give-and-take of these clean, bright entertainments and had ceased to think it worth while to make any comment when there was a certain liveliness.

'Ladies and gentlemen,' said old Beefy, 'the next item on the programme was to have been Songs by Miss Cora Bellinger, the well-known operatic soprano. I have just received a telephone-message from Miss Bellinger, saying that her car has broken down. She is, however, on her way here in a cab and will arrive shortly. Meanwhile, our friend Mr Enoch Simpson will recite "Dangerous Dan McGrew".'

I clutched at Jeeves.

'Jeeves! You heard?'

'Yes, sir.'

'She wasn't there!'

'No, sir.'

'She saw nothing of Tuppy's Waterloo.'

'No, sir.'

'The whole bally scheme has blown a fuse.'

'Yes, sir.'

'Come, Jeeves,' I said, and those standing by wondered, no doubt, what had caused that clean-cut face
to grow so pale and set. 'I have been subjected to a
nervous strain unparalleled since the days of the early
Martyrs. I have lost pounds in weight and permanently
injured my entire system. I have gone through an ordeal,
the recollection of which will make me wake up scream-
ing in the night for months to come. And all for nothing.
Let us go.'

'If you have no objection, sir, I would like to witness
the remainder of the entertainment.'

'Suit yourself, Jeeves,' I said moodily. 'Personally, my
heart is dead and I am going to look in at the Goat and
Grapes for another of their cyanide specials and then
home.'

It must have been about half-past ten, and I was in the
old sitting-room sombrely sucking down a more or less
final restorative, when the front door bell rang, and
there on the mat was young Tuppy. He looked like a
man who has passed through some great experience
and stood face to face with his soul. He had the begin-
nings of a black eye.

'Oh, hullo, Bertie,' said young Tuppy.

He came in, and hovered about the mantelpiece as if
he were looking for things to fiddle with and break.

'I've just been singing at Beefy Bingham's entertainment,' he said after a pause.

'Oh?' I said. 'How did you go?'

'Like a breeze,' said young Tuppy. 'Held them
spellbound.'

'Knocked 'em, eh?'

'Cold,' said young Tuppy. 'Not a dry eye.'

And this, mark you, a man who had had a good upbringing and had, no doubt, spent years at his mother's knee being taught to tell the truth.

'I suppose Miss Bellinger is pleased?'

'Oh, yes. Delighted.'

'So now everything's all right?'

'Oh, quite.'

Tuppy paused.

'On the other hand, Bertie – '

'Yes?'

'Well, I've been thinking things over. Somehow I don't believe Miss Bellinger is the mate for me after all.'

'You don't?'

'No, I don't.'

'Why don't you?'

'Oh, I don't know. These things sort of flash on you. I respect Miss Bellinger, Bertie. I admire her. But – er – well, I can't help feeling now that a sweet, gentle girl – er – like your cousin Angela, for instance, Bertie, – would – er – in fact – well, what I came round for was to ask if you would 'phone Angela and find out how she reacts to the idea of coming out with me tonight to the Berkeley for a segment of supper and a spot of dancing.'

'Go ahead. There's the 'phone.'

'No, I'd rather you asked her, Bertie. What with one thing and another, if you paved the way – You see, there's just a chance that she may be – I mean, you know how misunderstandings occur – and – well, what I'm driving at, Bertie, old man, is that I'd rather you surged round and did a bit of paving, if you don't mind.'

I went to the 'phone and called up Aunt Dahlia's.

'She says come right along,' I said.

'Tell her,' said Tuppy in a devout sort of voice, 'that I will be with her in something under a couple of ticks.'

He had barely biffed, when I heard a click in the keyhole and a soft padding in the passage without.

'Jeeves,' I called.

'Sir?' said Jeeves, manifesting himself.

'Jeeves, a remarkably rummy thing has happened. Mr Glossop has just been here. He tells me that it is all off between him and Miss Bellinger.'

'Yes, sir.'

'You don't seem surprised.'

'No, sir. I confess I had anticipated some such eventuality.'

'Eh? What gave you that idea?'

'It came to me, sir, when I observed Miss Bellinger strike Mr Glossop in the eye.'

'Strike him!'

'Yes, sir.'

'In the eye?'

'The right eye, sir.'

I clutched the brow.

'What on earth made her do that?'

'I fancy she was a little upset, sir, at the reception accorded to her singing.'

'Great Scott! Don't tell me she got the bird, too?'

'Yes, sir.'

'But why? She's got a red-hot voice.'

'Yes, sir. But I think the audience resented her choice of a song.'

'Jeeves!' Reason was beginning to do a bit of tottering on its throne. 'You aren't going to stand there and tell me that Miss Bellinger sang "Sonny Boy", too!'

'Yes, sir. And – rashly, in my opinion – brought a large doll on to the platform to sing it to. The audience affected to mistake it for a ventriloquist's dummy, and there was some little disturbance.'

'But, Jeeves, what a coincidence!'

'Not altogether, sir. I ventured to take the liberty of accosting Miss Bellinger on her arrival at the hall and recalling myself to her recollection. I then said that Mr Glossop had asked me to request her that as a particular favour to him – the song being a favourite of his – she would sing "Sonny Boy". And when she found that you and Mr Glossop had also sung the song immediately before her, I rather fancy that she supposed that she had been made the victim of a practical pleasantry by Mr Glossop. Will there be anything further, sir?'

'No, thanks.'

'Good night, sir.'

'Good night, Jeeves,' I said reverently.

=8=
EPISODE OF THE DOG McINTOSH

I was jerked from the dreamless by a sound like the rolling of distant thunder; and, in the mists of sleep clearing away, was enabled to diagnose this and trace it to its source. It was my Aunt Agatha's dog, McIntosh, scratching at the door. The above, an Aberdeen terrier of weak intellect, had been left in my charge by the old relative while she went off to Aix-les-Bains to take the cure, and I had never been able to make it see eye to eye with me on the subject of early rising. Although a glance at my watch informed me that it was barely ten, here was the animal absolutely up and about.

I pressed the bell, and presently in shimmered Jeeves, complete with tea-tray and preceded by dog, which leaped upon the bed, licked me smartly in the right eye, and immediately curled up and fell into a deep slumber. And where the sense is in getting up at some ungodly hour of the morning and coming scratching at people's doors, when you intend at the first opportunity to go to sleep again, beats me. Nevertheless, every day for the last five weeks this looney hound had pursued the same policy, and I confess I was getting a bid fed.

There were one or two letters on the tray; and, having slipped a refreshing half-cupful into the abyss, I felt equal to dealing with them. The one on top was from my Aunt Agatha.

'Ha!' I said.

'Sir?'

'I said "Ha!" Jeeves. And I meant "Ha!" I was registering relief. My Aunt Agatha returns this evening. She will be at her town residence between the hours of six and seven, and she expects to find McIntosh waiting for her on the mat.'

'Indeed, sir? I shall miss the little fellow.'

'I, too, Jeeves. Despite his habit of rising with the milk and being hearty before breakfast, there is sterling stuff in McIntosh. Nevertheless, I cannot but feel relieved at the prospect of shooting him back to the old home. It has been a guardianship fraught with anxiety. You know what my Aunt Agatha is. She lavishes on that dog a love which might better be bestowed on a nephew: and if the slightest thing had gone wrong with him while I was *in loco parentis*; if, while in my charge, he had developed rabies or staggers or the botts, I should have been blamed.'

'Very true, sir.'

'And, as you are aware, London is not big enough to hold Aunt Agatha and anybody she happens to be blaming.'

I had opened the second letter, and was giving it the eye.

'Ha!' I said.

'Sir?'

'Once again "Ha!" Jeeves, but this time signifying mild surprise. This letter is from Miss Wickham.'

'Indeed, sir?'

I sensed – if that is the word I want – the note of concern in the man's voice, and I knew he was saying to himself "Is the young master about to slip?" You see, there was a time when the Wooster heart was to some extent what you might call ensnared by this

115

Roberta Wickham, and Jeeves had never approved of her. He considered her volatile and frivolous and more or less of a menace to man and beast. And events, I'm bound to say, had rather borne out his view.

'She wants me to give her lunch to-day.'

'Indeed, sir?'

'And two friends of hers.'

'Indeed, sir?'

'Here. At one-thirty.'

'Indeed, sir?'

I was piqued.

'Correct this parrot-complex, Jeeves,' I said, waving a slice of bread-and-butter rather sternly at the man. 'There is no need for you to stand there saying "Indeed, sir?" I know what you're thinking, and you're wrong. As far as Miss Wickham is concerned, Bertram Wooster is chilled steel. I see no earthly reason why I should not comply with this request. A Wooster may have ceased to love, but he can still be civil.'

'Very good, sir.'

'Employ the rest of the morning, then, in buzzing to and fro and collecting provender. The old King Wenceslas touch, Jeeves. You remember? Bring me fish and bring me fowl – '

'Bring me flesh and bring me wine, sir.'

'Just as you say. You know best. Oh, and roly-poly pudding, Jeeves.'

'Sir?'

'Roly-poly pudding with lots of jam in it. Miss Wickham specifically mentions this. Mysterious, what?'

'Extremely, sir.'

'Also oysters, ice-cream, and plenty of chocolates with that gooey, slithery stuff in the middle. Makes you sick to think of it, eh?'

'Yes, sir.'

'Me, too. But that's what she says. I think she must be on some kind of diet. Well, be that as it may, see to it, Jeeves, will you?'

'Yes, sir.'

'At one-thirty of the clock.'

'Very good, sir.'

'Very good, Jeeves.'

At half past twelve I took the dog McIntosh for his morning saunter in the Park; and, returning at about one-ten, found young Bobbie Wickham in the sitting-room, smoking a cigarette and chatting to Jeeves, who seemed a bit distant, I thought.

I have an idea I've told you about this Bobbie Wickham. She was the red-haired girl who let me down so disgracefully in the sinister affair of Tuppy Glossop and the hot-water bottle, that Christmas when I went to stay at Skeldings Hall, her mother's place in Hertfordshire. Her mother is Lady Wickham, who writes novels which, I believe, command a ready sale among those who like their literature pretty sloppy. A formidable old bird, rather like my Aunt Agatha in appearance. Bobbie does not resemble her, being constructed more on the lines of Clara Bow. She greeted me cordially as I entered – in fact, so cordially that I saw Jeeves pause at the door before biffing off to mix the cocktails and shoot me the sort of grave, warning look a wise old father might pass out to the effervescent son on seeing him going fairly strong with the local vamp. I nodded back, as much as to say "Chilled steel!" and he oozed out, leaving me to play the sparkling host.

'It was awfully sporting of you to give us this lunch, Bertie,' said Bobbie.

'Don't mention it, my dear old thing,' I said. 'Always a pleasure.'

'You got all the stuff I told you about?'

'The garbage, as specified, is in the kitchen. But since when have you become a roly-poly pudding addict?'

'That isn't for me. There's a small boy coming.'

'What!'

'I'm awfully sorry,' she said, noting my agitation. 'I know just how you feel, and I'm not going to pretend that this child isn't pretty near the edge. In fact, he has to be seen to be believed. But it's simply vital that he be cosseted and sucked up to and generally treated as the guest of honour, because everything depends on him.'

'How do you mean?'

'I'll tell you. You know mother?'

'Whose mother?'

'My mother.'

'Oh, yes. I thought you meant the kid's mother.'

'He hasn't got a mother. Only a father, who is a big theatrical manager in America. I met him at a party the other night.'

'The father?'

'Yes, the father.'

'Not the kid?'

'No, not the kid.'

'Right. All clear so far. Proceed.'

'Well, mother – my mother – has dramatized one of her novels and when I met this father, this theatrical manager father, and, between ourselves, made rather a hit with him, I said to myself, "Why not?" '

'Why not what?'

'Why not plant mother's play on him.'

'Your mother's play?'

'Yes, not his mother's play. He is like his son, he hasn't got a mother, either.'

'These things run in families, don't they?'

'You see, Bertie, what with one thing and another,

118

my stock isn't very high with mother just now. There was that matter of my smashing up the car – oh, and several things. So I thought, here is where I get a chance to put myself right. I cooed to old Blumenfeld – '

'Name sounds familiar.'

'Oh, yes, he's a big man over in America. He has come to London to see if there's anything in the play line worth buying. So I cooed to him a goodish bit and then asked him if he would listen to mother's play. He said he would, so I asked him to come to lunch and I'd read it to him.'

'You're going to read your mother's play – here?' I said, paling.

'Yes.'

'My God!'

'I know what you mean,' she said. 'I admit it's pretty sticky stuff. But I have an idea that I shall put it over. It all depends on how the kid likes it. You see, old Blumenfeld, for some reason always banks on his verdict. I suppose he thinks the child's intelligence is exactly the same as an average audience's and – '

I uttered a slight yelp, causing Jeeves, who had entered with cocktails, to look at me in a pained sort of way. I had remembered.

'Jeeves!'

'Sir?'

'Do you recollect, when we were in New York, a dish-faced kid of the name of Blumenfeld who on a memorable occasion snootered Cyril Bassington-Bassington when the latter tried to go on the stage?'

'Very vividly, sir.'

'Well, prepare yourself for a shock. He's coming to lunch.'

'Indeed, sir?'

'I'm glad you can speak in that light, careless way. I

only met the young stoup of arsenic for a few brief minutes, but I don't mind telling you the prospect of hob-nobbing with him again makes me tremble like a leaf.'

'Indeed, sir?'

'Don't keep saying "Indeed, sir?" You have seen this kid in action and you know what he's like. He told Cyril Bassington-Bassington, a fellow to whom he had never been formally introduced, that he had a face like a fish. And this not thirty seconds after their initial meeting. I give you fair warning that, if he tells me I have a face like a fish, I shall clump his head.'

'Bertie!' cried the Wickham, contorted with anguish and apprehension and what not.

'Yes, I shall.'

'Then you'll simply ruin the whole thing.'

'I don't care. We Woosters have our pride.'

'Perhaps the young gentleman will not notice that you have a face like a fish, sir,' suggested Jeeves.

'Ah! There's that, of course.'

'But we can't just trust to luck,' said Bobbie. 'It's probably the first thing he will notice.'

'In that case, miss,' said Jeeves, 'it might be the best plan if Mr Wooster did not attend the luncheon.'

I beamed on the man. As always, he had found the way.

'But Mr Blumenfeld will think it so odd.'

'Well, tell him I'm eccentric. Tell him I have these moods, which come upon me quite suddenly, when I can't stand the sight of people. Tell him what you like.'

'He'll be offended.'

'Not half so offended as if I socked his son on the upper maxillary bone.'

'I really think it would be the best plan, miss.'

'Oh, all right,' said Bobbie. 'Push off, then. But I

wanted you to be here to listen to the play and laugh in the proper places.'

'I don't suppose there are any proper places,' I said. And with these words I reached the hall in two bounds, grabbed a hat, and made for the street. A cab was just pulling up at the door as I reached it, and inside it were Pop Blumenfeld and his foul son. With a slight sinking of the old heart, I saw that the kid had recognized me.

'Hullo!' he said.

'Hullo!' I said.

'Where are you off to?' said the kid.

'Ha, ha!' I said, and legged it for the great open spaces.

I lunched at the Drones, doing myself fairly well and lingering pretty considerably over coffee and cigarettes. At four o'clock I thought it would be safe to think about getting back; but, not wishing to take any chances, I went to the 'phone and rang up the flat.

'All clear, Jeeves?'

'Yes, sir.'

'Blumenfeld junior nowhere about?'

'No, sir.'

'Not hiding in any nook or cranny, what?'

'No, sir.'

'How did everything go off?'

'Quite satisfactory, I fancy, sir.'

'Was I missed?'

'I think Mr Blumenfeld and young Master Blumenfeld were somewhat surprised at your absence, sir. Apparently they encountered you as you were leaving the building.'

'They did. An awkward moment, Jeeves. The kid appeared to desire speech with me, but I laughed hollowly and passed on. Did they comment on this at all?'

'Yes, sir. Indeed, young Master Blumenfeld was somewhat outspoken.'

'What did he say?'

'I cannot recall his exact words, sir, but he drew a comparison between your mentality and that of a cuckoo.'

'A cuckoo, eh?'

'Yes, sir. To the bird's advantage.'

'He did, did he? Now you see how right I was to come away. Just one crack like that out of him face to face, and I should infallibly have done his upper maxillary a bit of no good. It was wise of you to suggest that I should lunch out.'

'Thank you, sir.'

'Well, the coast being clear, I will now return home.'

'Before you start, sir, perhaps you would ring Miss Wickham up. She instructed me to desire you to do so.'

'You mean she asked you to ask me?'

'Precisely, sir.'

'Right ho. And the number?'

'Sloane 8090. I fancy it is the residence of Miss Wickham's aunt, in Eaton Square.'

I got the number. And presently young Bobbie's voice came floating over the wire. From the *timbre* I gathered that she was extremely bucked.

'Hullo? Is that you, Bertie?'

'In person. What's the news?'

'Wonderful. Everything went off splendidly. The lunch was just right. The child stuffed himself to the eyebrows and got more and more amiable, till by the time he had had his third go of ice-cream he was ready to say that any play – even one of mother's – was the goods. I fired it at him before he could come out from under the influence, and he sat there absorbing it in a sort of gorged way, and at the end old Blumenfeld said

"Well, sonny, how about it?" and the child gave a sort of faint smile, as if he was thinking about roly-poly pudding, and said "O.K., pop," and that's all there was to it. Old Blumenfeld has taken him off to the movies, and I'm to look in at the Savoy at five-thirty to sign the contract. I've just been talking to mother on the 'phone, and she's quite consumedly braced.'

'Terrific!'

'I knew you'd be pleased. Oh, Bertie, there's just one other thing. You remember saying to me once that there wasn't anything in the world you wouldn't do for me?'

I paused a trifle warily. It is true that I had expressed myself in some such terms as she had indicated, but that was before the affair of Tuppy and the hot-water bottle, and in the calmer frame of mind induced by that episode I wasn't feeling quite so spacious. You know how it is. Love's flame flickers and dies, Reason returns to her throne, and you aren't nearly as ready to hop about and jump through hoops as in the first pristine glow of the divine passion.

'What do you want me to do?'

'Well, it's nothing I actually want you to do. It's something I've done that I hope you won't be sticky about. Just before I began reading the play, that dog of yours, the Aberdeen terrier, came into the room. The child Blumenfeld was very much taken with it and said he wished he had a dog like that, looking at me in a meaning sort of way. So naturally, I had to say "Oh, I'll give you this one!" '

I swayed somewhat.

'You. . . . you. . . . What was that?'

'I gave him the dog. I knew you wouldn't mind. You see, it was vital to keep cosseting him. If I'd refused, he would have cut up rough and all that roly-poly pudding and stuff would have been thrown away. You see – '

I hung up. The jaw had fallen, the eyes were protruding. I tottered from the booth and, reeling out of the club, hailed a taxi. I got to the flat and yelled for Jeeves.

'Jeeves!'

'Sir?'

'Do you know what?'

'No, sir.'

'The dog... my Aunt Agatha's dog... McIntosh...'

'I have not seen him for some little while, sir. He left me after the conclusion of luncheon. Possibly he's in your bedroom.'

'Yes, and possibly he jolly dashed well isn't. If you want to know where he is, he's in a suite at the Savoy.'

'Sir?'

'Miss Wickham has just told me she gave him to Blumenfeld junior.'

'Sir?'

'Gave him to Jumenfeld blunior, I tell you. As a present. As a gift. With warm personal regards.'

'What was her motive in doing that, sir?'

'I explained the circs. Jeeves did a bit of respectful tongue-clicking.

'I have always maintained, if you will remember, sir,' he said, when I had finished, 'that Miss Wickham, though a charming young lady – '

'Yes, Yes, never mind about that. What are we going to do? That's the point. Aunt Agatha is due back between the hours of six and seven. She will find herself short one Aberdeen terrier. And, as she will probably have been considerably sea-sick all the way over, you will readily perceive, Jeeves, that, when I break the news that her dog has been given away to a total stranger, I shall find her in no mood of gentle charity.'

'I see, sir, most disturbing.'

124

'What did you say it was?'

'Most disturbing, sir.'

I snorted a trifle.

'Oh?' I said. 'And I suppose, if you had been in San Francisco when the earthquake started, you would just have lifted up your finger and said "Tweet, tweet! Shush, shush! Now, now! Come, come!" The English language, they used to tell me at school, is the richest in the world, crammed full from end to end with about a million red-hot adjectives. Yet the only one you can find to describe this ghastly business is the adjective "disturbing". It is not disturbing, Jeeves. It is . . . what's the word I want?'

'Cataclysmal, sir.'

'I shouldn't wonder. Well, what's to be done?'

'I will bring you a whisky-and-soda, sir.'

'What's the good of that?'

'It will refresh you, sir. And in the meantime, if it is your wish, I will give the matter consideration.'

'Carry on.'

'Very good, sir. I assume that it is not your desire to do anything that may in any way jeopardize the cordial relations which now exist between Miss Wickham and Mr and Master Blumenfeld?'

'Eh?'

'You would not, for example, contemplate proceeding to the Savoy Hotel and demanding the return of the dog?'

It was a tempting thought, but I shook the old onion firmly. There are things which a Wooster can do and things which, if you follow me, a Wooster cannot do. The procedure which he had indicated would undoubtedly have brought home the bacon, but the thwarted kid would have been bound to turn nasty and change his mind about the play. And, while I didn't think that

125

any drama written by Bobbie's mother was likely to do
the theatre-going public much good, I couldn't dash the
cup of happiness, so to speak, from the blighted girl's
lips, as it were. *Noblesse oblige* about sums the thing
up.

'No, Jeeves,' I said. 'But if you can think of some
way by which I can oil privily into the suite and sneak
the animal out of it without causing any hard feelings,
spill it.'

'I will endeavour to do so, sir.'

'Snap into it, then, without delay. They say fish are
good for the brain. Have a go at the sardines and come
back and report.'

'Very good, sir.'

It was about ten minutes later that he entered the
presence once more.

'I fancy, sir – '

'Yes, Jeeves?'

'I rather fancy, sir, that I have discovered a plan of
action.'

'Or scheme.'

'Or scheme, sir. A plan of action or scheme which
will meet the situation. If I understood you rightly, sir,
Mr and Master Blumenfeld have attended a motion-
picture performance?'

'Correct.'

'In which case, they should not return to the hotel
before five-fifteen?'

'Correct once more. Miss Wickham is scheduled to
blow in at five-thirty to sign the contract.'

'The suite, therefore, is presently unoccupied.'

'Except for McIntosh.'

'Except for McIntosh, sir. Everything, accordingly,
must depend on whether Mr Blumenfeld left instructions that, in the event of her arriving before he did,

Miss Wickham was to be shown straight up to the suite, to await his return.'

'Why does everything depend on that?'

'Should he have done so, the matter becomes quite simple. All that is necessary is that Miss Wickham shall present herself at the hotel at five o'clock. She will go up to the suite. You will also have arrived at the hotel at five, sir, and will have made your way to the corridor outside the suite. If Mr and Master Blumenfeld have not returned, Miss Wickham will open the door and come out and you will go in, secure the dog, and take your departure.'

I stared at the man.

'How many tins of sardines did you eat, Jeeves?'

'None, sir. I am not fond of sardines.'

'You man, you thought of this great, this ripe, this amazing scheme entirely without the impetus given to the brain by fish?'

'Yes, sir.'

'You stand alone, Jeeves.'

'Thank you sir.'

'But I say!'

'Sir?'

'Suppose the dog won't come away with me? You know how meagre his intelligence is. By this time, especially when he's got used to a new place, he may have forgotten me completely and will look on me as a perfect stranger.'

'I had thought of that, sir. The most judicious move will be for you to sprinkle your trousers with aniseed.'

'Aniseed?'

'Yes, sir. It is extensively used in the dog-stealing industry.'

'But Jeeves . . . dash it . . . aniseed?'

'I consider it essential, sir.'

'But where do you get the stuff?'

'At any chemist's, sir. If you will go out now and procure a small bottle, I will be telephoning to Miss Wickham to apprise her of the contemplated arrangements and ascertain whether she is to be admitted to the suite.'

I don't know what the record is for popping out and buying aniseed, but I should think I hold it. The thought of Aunt Agatha getting nearer and nearer to the Metropolis every minute induced a rare burst of spped. I was back at the flat so quick that I nearly met myself coming out.

Jeeves had good news.

'Everything is perfectly satisfactory, sir. Mr Blumenfeld did leave instructions that Miss Wickham was to be admitted to his suite. The young lady is now on her way to the hotel. By the time you reach it, you will find her there.'

You know, whatever you may say about old Jeeves – and I, for one, have never wavered in my opinion that his views on shirts for evening wear are hidebound and reactionary to a degree – you've got to admit that the man can plan a campaign. Napoleon could have taken his correspondence course. When he sketches out a scheme, all you have to do is to follow it in every detail, and there you are.

On the present occasion everything went absolutely according to plan, I had never realized before that dog-stealing could be so simple, having always regarded it rather as something that called for the ice-cool brain and the nerve of steel. I see now that a child can do it, if directed by Jeeves. I got to the hotel, sneaked up the stairs, hung about in the corridor trying to look like a potted palm in case anybody came along, and presently the door of the suite opened and Bobbie appeared, and suddenly, as I approached, out shot McIntosh, sniffing passionately, and the next moment his nose was up against my Spring trouserings, and he was drinking me in with every evidence of enjoyment. If I had been a bird that had been dead about five days, he could not have nuzzled me more heartily. Aniseed isn't a scent that I care for particularly myself, but it seemed to speak straight to the deeps of McIntosh's soul.

The connection, as it were, having been established in this manner, the rest was simple. I merely withdrew, followed by the animal in the order named. We passed down the stairs in good shape, self reeking to heaven and animal inhaling the bouquet, and after a few anxious moments were safe in a cab, homeward bound. As smooth a bit of work as London had seen that day.

Arrived at the flat, I handed McIntosh to Jeeves and instructed him to shut him up in the bathroom or somewhere where the spell cast by my trousers would cease to operate. This done, I again paid the man a marked tribute.

'Jeeves,' I said, 'I have had occasion to express the view before, and I now express it again fearlessly – you stand in a class of your own.'

'Thank you very much, sir. I am glad that everything proceeded satisfactorily.'

'The festivities went like a breeze from start to finish. Tell me, were you always like this, or did it come on suddenly?'

'Sir?'

'The brain. The grey matter. Were you an outstanding brilliant boy?'

'My mother thought me intelligent, sir.'

'You can't go by that. My mother thought *me* intelligent. Anyway, setting that aside for the moment, would a fiver be any use to you?'

'Thank you very much, sir.'

'Not that a fiver begins to cover it. Figure to yourself, Jeeves – try to envisage, if you follow what I mean, the probable behaviour of my Aunt Agatha if I had gone to her between the hours of six and seven and told her that McIntosh had passed out of the picture. I should have had to leave London and grow a beard.'

'I can readily imagine, sir, that she would have been somewhat perturbed.'

'She would. And on the occasions when my Aunt Agatha is perturbed heroes dive down drain-pipes to get out of her way. However, as it is, all has ended happily. . . . Oh, great Scott!'

'Sir?'

I hesitated. It seemed a shame to cast a damper on the man just when he had extended himself so notably in the cause, but it had to be done.

'You've overlooked something, Jeeves.'

'Surely not, sir?'

'Yes, Jeeves, I regret to say that the late scheme or plan of action, while gilt-edged as far as I am concerned, has rather landed Miss Wickham in the cart.'

'In what way, sir?'

'Why, don't you see that, if they know that she was in the suite at the time of the outrage, the Blumenfelds, father and son, will instantly assume that she was mixed up in McIntosh's disappearance, with the result that in their pique and chagrin they will call off the deal about the play? I'm surprised at you not spotting that, Jeeves. You'd have done much better to eat those sardines, as I advised.'

I waggled my head rather sadly, and at this moment there was a ring at the front-door bell. And not an ordinary ring, mind you, but one of those resounding peals that suggest that somebody with a high blood-pressure and a grievance stands without. I leaped in my tracks. My busy afternoon had left the old nervous system not quite in mid-season form.

'Good Lord, Jeeves!'

'Somebody at the door, sir.'

'Yes.'

'Probably Mr Blumenfield, senior, sir.'

'What!'

'He rang up on the telephone, sir, shortly before you returned, to say that he was about to pay you a call.'

'You don't mean that?'

'Yes, sir.'

'Advise me, Jeeves.'

'I fancy the most judicious procedure would be for you to conceal yourself behind the settee, sir.'

I saw that his advice was good. I had never met this Blumenfield socially, but I had seen him from afar on the occasion when he and Cyril Bassington-Bassington had had their falling out, and he hadn't struck me then as a bloke with whom, if in one of his emotional moods, it would be at all agreeable to be shut up in a small room. A large, round, flat, overflowing bird, who might quite easily, if stirred, fall on a fellow and flatten him to the carpet.

So I nestled behind the settee, and in about five seconds there was a sound like a mighty, rushing wind and something extraordinarily substantial bounded into the sitting-room.

'This guy, Wooster,' bellowed a voice that had been strengthened by a lifetime of ticking actors off at dress-rehearsals from the back of the theatre.

'Where is he?'

Jeeves continued suave.

131

'I could not say, sir.'

'He's sneaked my son's dog.'

'Indeed, sir?'

'Walked into my suite as cool as dammit and took the animal away.'

'Most disturbing, sir.'

'And you don't know where he is?'

'Mr Wooster may be anywhere, sir. He is uncertain in his movements.'

The bloke Blumenfeld gave a loud sniff.

'Odd smell here!'

'Yes, sir?'

'What is it?'

'Aniseed, sir.'

'Aniseed?'

'Yes, sir. Mr Wooster sprinkles it on his trousers.'

'Sprinkles it on his trousers?'

'Yes, sir.'

'What on earth does he do that for?'

'I could not say, sir. Mr Wooster's motives are always somewhat hard to follow. He is eccentric.'

'Eccentric? He must be a loony.'

'Yes, sir.'

'You mean he is?'

'Yes, sir!'

There was a pause. A long one.

'Oh?' said old Blumenfeld, and it seemed to me that a good deal of what you might call the vim had gone out of his voice.

He paused again.

'Not *dangerous*?'

'Yes, sir, when roused.'

'Er – what rouses him chiefly?'

'One of Mr Wooster's peculiarities is that he does

not like the sight of gentlemen of full habit, sir. They seem to infuriate him.'

'You mean, fat men?'

'Yes, sir.'

'Why?'

'One cannot say, sir.'

There was another pause.

'*I'm* fat!' said old Blumenfeld in a rather pensive sort of voice.

'I would not venture to suggest it myself, sir, but as you say so. . . . You may recollect that, on being informed that you were to be a member of the luncheon party, Mr Wooster, doubting his power of self-control, refused to be present.'

'That's right. He went rushing out just as I arrived. I thought it odd at the time. My son thought it odd. We both thought it odd.'

'Yes, sir. Mr Wooster, I imagine, wished to avoid any possible unpleasantness, such as has occurred before. . . . With regard to the smell of aniseed, sir, I fancy I have now located it. Unless I am mistaken it proceeds from behind the settee. No doubt Mr Wooster is sleeping there.'

'Doing what?'

'Sleeping, sir.'

'Does he often sleep on the floor?'

'Most afternoons, sir. Would you desire me to wake him?'

'No!'

'I thought you had something that you wished to say to Mr Wooster, sir.'

Old Blumenfeld drew a deep breath. 'So did I,' he said. 'But I find I haven't. Just get me alive out of here, that's all I ask.'

I heard the door close, and a little while later the

front door banged. I crawled out. It hadn't been any too cosy behind the settee, and I was glad to be elsewhere. Jeeves came trickling back.

'Gone, Jeeves?'

'Yes, sir.'

I bestowed an approving look on him.

'One of your best efforts, Jeeves.'

'Thank you, sir.'

'But what beats me is why he ever came here. What made him think that I had sneaked McIntosh away?'

'I took the liberty of recommending Miss Wickham to tell Mr Blumenfeld that she had observed you removing the animal from his suite, sir. The point which you raised regarding the possibility of her being suspected of complicity in the affair had not escaped me. It seemed to me that this would establish her solidly in Mr Blumenfeld's good opinion.'

'I see. Risky, of course, but possibly justified. Yes, on the whole, justified. What's that you've got there?'

'A five pound note, sir.'

'Ah, the one I gave you?'

'No, sir. The one Mr Blumenfeld gave me.'

'Eh? Why did he give you a fiver?'

'He very kindly presented it to me on my handing him the dog, sir.'

I gaped at the man.

'You don't mean to say – ?'

'Not McIntosh, sir. McIntosh is at present in my bedroom. This was another animal of the same species which I purchased at the shop in Bond Street during your absence. Except to the eye of love, one Aberdeen terrier looks very much like another Aberdeen terrier, sir. Mr Blumenfeld, I am happy to say, did not detect the innocent subterfuge.'

'Jeeves,' I said – and I am not ashamed to confess

that there was a spot of chokiness in the voice – 'there is none like you, none.'

'Thank you very much, sir.'

'Owing solely to the fact that your head bulges in unexpected spots, thus enabling you to do about twice as much bright thinking in any given time as any other two men in existence, happiness, you might say, reigns supreme. Aunt Agatha is on velvet, I am on velvet, the Wickhams, mother and daughter, are on velvet, the Blumenfelds, father and son, are on velvet. As far as the eye can reach, a solid mass of humanity, owing to you, all on velvet. A fiver is not sufficient, Jeeves. If I thought the world thought that Bertram Wooster thought a measly five pounds an adequate reward for such services as yours, I should never hold my head up again. Have another?'

'Thank you, sir.'

'And one more?'

'Thank you very much, sir.'

'And a third for luck?'

'Really, sir, I am exceedingly obliged. Excuse me, sir, I fancy I heard the telephone.'

He pushed out into the hall, and I heard him doing a good deal of the "Yes, madam", "Certainly, madam!" stuff. Then he came back.

'Mrs Spencer Gregson on the telephone, sir.'

'Aunt Agatha?'

'Yes, sir. Speaking from Victoria Station. She desires to communicate with you with reference to the dog McIntosh. I gather that she wishes to hear from your own lips that all is well with the little fellow, sir.'

I straightened the tie. I pulled down the waistcoat. I shot the cuffs. I felt absolutely all-righto.

'Lead me to her,' I said.

=9=
COMRADE BINGO

The thing really started in the Park – at the Marble Arch end – where weird birds of every description collect on Sunday afternoons and stand on soap-boxes and make speeches. It isn't often you'll find me there, but it so happened that, on the Sabbath after my return to the good old Metrop. I had a call to pay in Manchester Square, and, taking a stroll round in that direction so as not to arrive too early, I found myself right in the middle of it.

Now that the Empire isn't the place it was, I always think the Park on a Sunday is the centre of London, if you know what I mean. I mean to say, that's the spot that makes the returned exile really sure he's back again. After what you might call my enforced sojourn in New York I'm bound to say that I stood there fairly lapping it all up. It did me good to listen to the lads giving tongue and realize that all had ended happily and Bertram was home again.

On the edge of the mob farthest away from me a gang of top-hatted chappies were starting an open-air missionary service; nearer at hand an atheist was letting himself go with a good deal of vim, though handicapped a bit by having no roof to his mouth; while in front of me there stood a little group of serious thinkers with a banner labelled "Heralds of the Red Dawn"; and as I came up, one of the heralds, a bearded egg in a slouch hat and a tweed suit, was slipping it into the Idle Rich

with such breadth and vigour that I paused for a
moment to get an earful. While I was standing there
somebody spoke to me.

'Mr Wooster, surely?'

Stout chappie. Couldn't place him for a second. Then
I got him. Bingo Little's uncle, the one I had lunch with
at the time when young Bingo was in love with that
waitress at the Piccadilly bun-shop. No wonder I hadn't
recognized him at first. When I had seen him last he
had been a rather sloppy old gentleman – coming down
to lunch, I remember, in carpet slippers and a velvet
smoking-jacket; whereas now dapper simply wasn't the
word. He absolutely gleamed in the sunlight in a silk
hat, morning coat, lavender spats and sponge-bag trousers, as now worn. Dressy to a degree.

'Oh, hallo!' I said. 'Going strong?'

'I am in excellent health, I thank you. And you?'

'In the pink. Just been over to America.'

'Ah! Collecting local colour for one of your delightful
romances?'

'Eh?' I had to think a bit before I got on to what he
meant. 'Oh, no,' I said. 'Just felt I needed a change.
Seen anything of Bingo lately?' I asked quickly, being
desirous of heading the old thing off what you might
call the literary side of life.

'Bingo?'

'Your nephew.'

'Oh, Richard? No, not very recently. Since my marriage a little coolness seems to have sprung up.'

'Sorry to hear that. So you've married since I saw
you, what? Mrs Little all right?'

'My wife is happily robust. But – er – *not* Mrs Little.
Since we last met a gracious Sovereign has been pleased
to bestow on me a signal mark of his favour in the

shape of – ah – a peerage. On the publication of the last Honours List I became Lord Bittlesham.'

'By Jove! Really? I say, heartiest congratulations. That's the stuff to give the troops, what? Lord Bittlesham?' I said. 'Why, you're the owner of Ocean Breeze.'

'Yes. Marriage has enlarged my horizon in many directions. My wife is interested in horse-racing, and I now maintain a small stable. I understand that Ocean Breeze is fancied, as I am told the expression is, for a race which will take place at the end of the month at Goodwood, the Duke of Richmond's seat in Sussex.'

'The Goodwood Cup. Rather! I've got my chemise on it for one.'

'Indeed? Well, I trust the animal will justify your confidence. I know little of these matters myself, by my wife tells me that it is regarded in knowledgeable circles as what I believe is termed a snip.'

At this moment I suddenly noticed that the audience was gazing in our direction with a good deal of interest, and I saw that the bearded chappie was pointing at us.

'Yes, look at them! Drink them in!' he was yelling, his voice rising above the perpetual-motion fellow's and beating the missionary service all to nothing. 'There you see two typical members of the class which has downtrodden the poor for centuries. Idlers! Non-producers! Look at the tall thin one with the face like a motor-mascot. Has he ever done an honest day's work in his life? No! A prowler, a trifler, and a blood-sucker! And I bet he still owes his tailor for those trousers!'

He seemed to me to be verging on the personal, and I didn't think a lot of it. Old Bittlesham, on the other hand, was pleased and amused.

'A great gift of expression these fellows have,' he chuckled. 'Very trenchant.'

'And the fat one!' proceeded the chappie. 'Don't miss

him. Do you know who that is? That's Lord Bittlesham! One of the worst. What has he ever done except eat four square meals a day! His god is his belly, and he sacrifices burnt-offerings to it. If you opened that man now you would find enough lunch to support ten working-class families for a week.'

'You know, that's rather well put,' I said, but the old boy didn't seem to see it. He had turned a brightish magenta and was bubbling like a kettle on the boil.

'Come away, Mr Wooster,' he said. 'I am the last man to oppose the right of free speech, but I refuse to listen to this vulgar abuse any longer.'

We legged it with quiet dignity, the chappie pursuing us with his foul innuendoes to the last. Dashed embarrassing.

Next day I looked in at the club, and found young Bingo in the smoking-room.

'Hallo, Bingo,' I said, toddling over to his corner full of *bonhomie*, for I was glad to see the chump. 'How's the boy?'

'Jogging along.'

'I saw your uncle yesterday.'

Young Bingo unleashed a grin that split his face in half.

'I know you did, you trifler. Well, sit down, old thing, and suck a bit of blood. How's the prowling these days?'

'Good Lord! You weren't there!'

'Yes, I was.'

'I didn't see you.'

'Yes, you did. But perhaps you didn't recognize me in the shrubbery.'

'The shrubbery?'

'The beard, my boy. Worth every penny I paid for it.

Defies detection. Of course, it's a nuisance having people shouting "Beaver!" at you all the time, but one's got to put up with that.'

I goggled at him.

'I don't understand.'

'It's a long story. Have a martini or a small gore-and-soda, and I'll tell you all about it. Before we start, give me your honest opinion. Isn't she the most wonderful girl you ever saw in your puff?'

He had produced a photograph from somewhere, like a conjurer taking a rabbit out of a hat, and was waving it in front of me. It appeared to be a female of sorts, all eyes and teeth.

'Oh, Great Scott!' I said. 'Don't tell me you're in love again.'

He seemed aggrieved.

'What do you mean – again?'

'Well, to my certain knowledge you've been in love with at least half a dozen girls since the spring, and it's only July now. There was that waitress and Honoria Glossop and – '

'Oh, tush! Not to say pish! Those girls? Mere passing fancies. This is the real thing.'

'Where did you meet her?'

'On top of a bus. Her name is Charlotte Corday Rowbotham.'

'My God!'

'It's not her fault, poor child. Her father had her christened that because he's all for the Revolution, and it seems that the original Charlotte Corday used to go about stabbing oppressors in their baths, which entitles her to consideration and respect. You must meet old Rowbotham, Bertie. A delightful chap. Wants to massacre the *bourgeoisie*, sack Park Lane and disembowel the hereditary aristocracy. Well, nothing could be fairer than that, what? But about Charlotte. We were on top of the bus, and it started to rain. I offered her my umbrella, and we chatted of this and that. I fell in love and got her address, and a couple of days later I bought the beard and toddled round and met the family.'

'But why the beard?'

'Well, she had told me all about her father on the bus, and I saw that to get any footing at all in the home I should have to join these Red Dawn blighters; and naturally, if I was to make speeches in the Park, where at any moment I might run into a dozen people I knew, something in the nature of a disguise was indicated. So I bought the beard, and, by Jove, old boy, I've become dashed attached to the thing. When I take it off to come in here, for instance, I feel absolutely nude. It's done me a lot of good with old Rowbotham. He thinks I'm a Bolshevist of sorts who has to go about disguised because of the police. You really must meet old Rowbotham, Bertie. I tell you what, are you doing anything tomorrow afternoon?'

'Nothing special. Why?'

'Good! Then you can have us all to eat at your flat. I had promised to take the crowd to Lyons' Popular Café after a meeting we're holding down in Lambeth, but I can save money this way; and, believe me, laddie, nowadays, as far as I'm concerned, a penny saved is a penny earned. My uncle told you he'd got married?'

'Yes. And he said there was a coolness between you.'

'Coolness? I'm down to zero. Ever since he married he's been launching out in every direction and economizing on *me*. I suppose that peerage cost the old devil the deuce of a sum. Even baronetcies have gone up frightfully nowadays, I'm told. And he's started a racing-stable. By the way, put your last collar stud on Ocean Breeze for the Goodwood Cup. It's a cert.'

'I'm going to.'

'It can't lose. I mean to win enough on it to marry Charlotte with. You're going to Goodwood, of course?'

'Rather!'

'So are we. We're holding a meeting on Cup day just outside the paddock.'

'But, I say, aren't you taking frightful risks? Your uncle's sure to be at Goodwood. Suppose he spots you? He'll be fed to the gills if he finds out that you're the fellow who ragged him in the Park.'

'How the deuce is he to find out? Use your intelligence, you prowling inhaler of red corpuscles. If he didn't spot me yesterday, why should he spot me at Goodwood? Well, thanks for your cordial invitation for to-morrow, old thing. We shall be delighted to accept. Do us well, laddie, and blessings shall reward you. By the way, I may have misled you by using the word "tea". None of your wafer slices of bread-and-butter. We're good trenchermen, we of the Revolution. What we shall require will be something on the order of scrambled eggs, muffins, jam, ham, cake and sardines. Expect us at five sharp.'

'But, I say, I'm not quite sure – '

'Yes, you are. Silly ass, don't you see that this is going to do you a bit of good when the Revolution breaks loose? When you see old Rowbotham sprinting up Piccadilly with a dripping knife in each hand, you'll be jolly thankful to be able to remind him that he once ate your tea and shrimps. There will be four of us, Charlotte, self, the old man, and Comrade Butt. I suppose he will insist on coming along.'

'Who the devil's Comrade Butt?'

'Did you notice a fellow standing on my left in our little troupe yesterday? Small, shrivelled chap. Looks like a haddock with lung-trouble. That's Butt. My rival, dash him. He's sort of semi-engaged to Charlotte at the moment. Till I came along he was the blue-eyed boy. He's got a voice like a foghorn, and old Rowbotham thinks a lot of him. But, hang it, if I can't thoroughly encompass this Butt and cut him out and put him where he belongs among the discards – well, I'm not the man I was, that's all. He may have a big voice, but he hasn't my gift of expression. Thank heaven I was once cox of my college boat. Well, I must be pushing now. I say, you don't know how I could raise fifty quid somehow, do you?'

'Why don't you work?'

'Work?' said young Bingo, surprised. 'What me? No, I shall have to think of some way. I must put at least fifty on Ocean Breeze. Well, see you to-morrow. God bless you, old sort, and don't forget the muffins.'

I don't know why, ever since I first knew him at school, I should have felt a rummy feeling of responsibility for young Bingo. I mean to say, he's not my son (thank goodness) or my brother, or anything like that. He's got absolutely no claim on me at all, and yet a large-sized chunk of my existence seems to be spent in fussing over him like a bally old hen and hauling him out of the soup. I suppose it must be some rare beauty in my nature or something. At any rate, this latest affair of his worried me. He seemed to be doing his best to marry into a family of pronounced loonies, and how the deuce he thought he was going to support even a mentally afflicted wife on nothing a year beat me. Old Bittlesham was bound to knock off his allowance if he did anything of the sort and, with a fellow like young Bingo, if you knocked off his allowance, you might just as well hit him on the head with an axe and make a clean job of it.

'Jeeves,' I said, when I got home, 'I'm worried.'

'Sir?'

'About Mr. Little. I won't tell you about it now, because he's bringing some friends of his to tea to-morrow, and then you will be able to judge for yourself. I want you to observe closely, Jeeves, and form your decision.'

'Very good, sir.'

'And about the tea. Get in some muffins.'

'Yes, sir.'

'And some jam, ham, cake, scrambled eggs, and five or six wagonloads of sardines.'

'Sardines, sir?' said Jeeves, with a shudder.

'Sardines.'

There was an awkward pause.

'Don't blame me, Jeeves,' I said. 'It isn't my fault.'

'No, sir.'

'Well, that's that.'

'Yes, sir.'

I could see the man was brooding tensely.

I've found, as a general rule in life, that the things you think are going to be the scaliest nearly always turn out not so bad after all; but it wasn't that way with Bingo's tea-party. From the moment he invited himself I felt that the thing was going to be blue round the edges, and it was. And I think the most gruesome part of the whole affair was the fact that, for the first time since I'd known him, I saw Jeeves come very near to being rattled. I suppose there's a chink in everyone's armour, and young Bingo found Jeeves's right at the drop of the flag when he breezed in with six inches or so of brown beard hanging on to his chin. I had forgotten to warn Jeeves about the beard, and it came on him absolutely out of a blue sky. I saw the man's jaw drop, and he clutched at the table for support. I don't blame him, mind you. Few people have ever looked fouler than young Bingo in the fungus. Jeeves paled a little; then the weakness passed and he was himself again. But I could see that he had been shaken.

Young Bingo was too busy introducing the mob to take much notice. They were a very C3 collection. Comrade Butt looked like one of the things that come out of dead trees after the rain; moth-eaten was the word I should have used to describe old Rowbotham; and as for Charlotte, she seemed to take me straight into another and a dreadful world. It wasn't that she was exactly bad-looking. In fact, if she had knocked off starchy foods and done Swedish exercises for a bit, she might have been quite tolerable. But there was too much of her. Billowy curves. Well-nourished, perhaps, expresses it best. And, while she may have had a heart of gold, the thing you noticed about her first was that she had a tooth of gold. I know that young Bingo, when in form, could fall in love with practically anything of the other sex; but this I couldn't see any excuse for him at all.

'My friend, Mr Wooster,' said Bingo, completing the ceremonial.

Old Rowbotham looked at me and then he looked round the room, and I could see he wasn't particularly braced. There's nothing of absolutely Oriental luxury about the old flat, but I have managed to make myself fairly comfortable, and I suppose the surroundings jarred him a bit.

'Mr Wooster?' said old Rowbotham. 'May I say Comrade Wooster?'

'I beg your pardon?'

'Are you of the movement?'

'Well – er –'

'Do you yearn for the Revolution?'

'Well, I don't know that I exactly yearn. I mean to say, as far as I can make out, the whole hub of the scheme seems to be to massacre coves like me; and I don't mind owning I'm not frightfully keen on the idea.'

'But I'm talking him round,' said Bingo. 'I'm wrestling with him. A few more treatments ought to do the trick.'

Old Rowbotham looked at me a bit doubtfully.

'Comrade Little has great eloquence,' he admitted.

'I think he talks something wonderful,' said the girl, and young Bingo shot a glance of such succulent devotion at her that I reeled in my tracks. It seemed to depress Comrade Butt a good deal too. He scowled at the carpet and said something about dancing on volcanoes.

'Tea is served, sir,' said Jeeves.

'Tea, pa!' said Charlotte, starting at the word like the old war-horse who hears the bugle; and we got down to it.

Funny how one changes as the years roll on. At school, I remember, I would cheerfully have sold my soul for scrambled eggs and sardines at five in the afternoon; but somehow, since reaching man's estate, I had rather dropped out of the habit; and I'm bound to admit I was appalled to a goodish extent at the way the sons and daughter of the Revolution shoved their heads down and went for the foodstuffs. Even Comrade Butt cast off his gloom for a space and immersed his whole being in scrambled eggs, only coming to the surface at intervals to grab another cup of tea. Presently the hot water gave out, and I turned to Jeeves.

'More hot water.'

'Very good, sir.'

'Hey! what's this? What's this?' Old Rowbotham had

lowered his cup and was eyeing us sternly. He tapped Jeeves on the shoulder. 'No servility, my lad; no servility!'

'I beg your pardon, sir?'

'Don't call me "sir". Call me Comrade. Do you know what you are, my lad? You're an obsolete relic of an exploded feudal system.'

'Very good, sir.'

'If there's one thing that makes my blood boil in my veins – '

'Have another sardine,' chipped in young Bingo – the first sensible thing he'd done since I had known him. Old Rowbotham took three and dropped the subject, and Jeeves drifted away. I could see by the look of his back what he felt.

At last, just as I was beginning to feel that it was going on for ever, the thing finished. I woke up to find the party getting ready to leave.

Sardines and about three quarts of tea had mellowed old Rowbotham. There was quite a genial look in his eye as he shook my hand.

'I must thank you for your hospitality, Comrade Wooster,' he said.

'Oh, not at all! Only too glad – '

'Hospitality?' snorted the man Butt, going off in my ear like a depth-charge. He was scowling in a morose sort of manner at young Bingo and the girl, who were giggling together by the window. 'I wonder the food didn't turn to ashes in our mouths! Eggs! Muffins! Sardines! All wrung from the bleeding lips of the starving poor!'

'Oh, I say! What a beastly idea!'

'I will send you some literature on the subject of the Cause,' said old Rowbotham. 'And soon, I hope, we shall see you at one of our little meetings.'

Jeeves came in to clear away, and found me sitting among the ruins. It was all very well for Comrade Butt to knock the food, but he had pretty well finished the ham; and if you had shoved the remainder of the jam into the bleeding lips of the starving poor it would hardly have made them sticky.

'Well, Jeeves,' I said, 'how about it?'

'I would prefer to express no opinion, sir,'

'Jeeves, Mr Little is in love with that female.'

'So I gathered, sir. She was slapping him in the passage.'

I clutched my brow.

'Slapping him?'

'Yes, sir. Roguishly.'

'Great Scott! I didn't know it had got as far as that. How did Comrade Butt seem to be taking it? Or perhaps he didn't see?'

'Yes, sir, he observed the entire proceedings. He struck me as extremely jealous.'

'I don't blame him. Jeeves, what are we to do?'

'I could not say, sir.'

'It's a bit thick.'

'Very much so, sir.'

And that was all the consolation I got from Jeeves.

=10=

BINGO HAS A BAD
GOODWOOD

I had promised to meet young Bingo next day, to tell
him what I thought of his infernal Charlotte, and I was
mooching slowly up St James's Street, trying to think
how the dickens I could explain to him, without hurting
his feelings, that I considered her one of the world's
foulest, when who should come toddling out of the
Devonshire Club but old Bittlesham and Bingo himself.
I hurried on and overtook them.

'What-ho!' I said.

The result of this simple greeting was a bit of a
shock. Old Bittlesham quivered from head to foot like a
poleaxed blancmange. His eyes were popping and his
face had gone sort of greenish.

'Mr Wooster!' He seemed to recover somewhat, as if
I wasn't the worst thing that could have happened to
him. 'You gave me a severe start.'

'Oh, sorry!'

'My uncle,' said young Bingo in a hushed, bedside
sort of voice, 'isn't feeling quite himself this morning.
He's had a threatening letter.'

'I go in fear of my life,' said old Bittlesham.

'Threatening letter?'

'Written,' said old Bittlesham, 'in an uneducated hand
and couched in terms of uncompromising menaces. Mr
Wooster, do you recall a sinister, bearded man who

149

assailed me in no measured terms in Hyde Park last Sunday?'

I jumped, and shot a look at young Bingo. The only expression on his face was one of grave, kindly concern.

'Why – ah – yes,' I said. 'Bearded man. Chap with a beard.'

'Could you identify him, if necessary?'

'Well, I – er – how do you mean?'

'The fact is, Bertie,' said Bingo, 'we think this man with the beard is at the bottom of all this business. I happened to be walking late last night through Pounceby Gardens, where Uncle Mortimer lives, and as I was passing the house a fellow came hurrying down the steps in a furtive sort of way. Probably he had just been shoving the letter in at the front door. I noticed that he had a beard. I didn't think any more of it, however, until this morning, when Uncle Mortimer showed me the letter he had received and told me about the chap in the Park. I'm going to make inquiries.'

'The police should be informed,' said Lord Bittlesham.

'No,' said young Bingo firmly, 'not at this stage of the proceedings. It would hamper me. Don't you worry, uncle; I think I can track this fellow down. You leave it all to me. I'll pop you into a taxi now, and go and talk it over with Bertie.'

'You're a good boy, Richard,' said old Bittlesham, and we put him in a passing cab and pushed off. I turned and looked young Bingo squarely in the eyeball.

'Did you send that letter?' I said.

'Rather! You ought to have seen it, Bertie! One of the best gent's ordinary threatening letters I ever wrote.'

'But where's the sense of it?'

'Bertie, my lad,' said Bingo, taking me earnestly by the coat-sleeve, 'I had an excellent reason. Posterity may

say of me what it will, but one thing it can never say –
that I have not a good solid business head. Look here!'
He waved a bit of paper in front of my eyes.

'Great Scott!' It was a cheque – an absolute, dashed
cheque for fifty of the best, signed Bittlesham, and made
out to the order of R. Little.

'What's that for?'

'Expenses,' said Bingo, pouching it. 'You don't suppose an investigation like this can be carried on for
nothing, do you! I now proceed to the bank and startle
them into a fit with it. Later I edge round to my bookie
and put the entire sum on Ocean Breeze. What you
want in situations of this kind, Bertie, is tact. If I had
gone to my uncle and asked him for fifty quid, would
I have got it? No! But by exercising tact – Oh! by the
way, what do you think of Charlotte?'

'Well – er – '

Young Bingo massaged my sleeve affectionately.

'I know, old man, I know. Don't try to find words.
She bowled you over, eh? Left you speechless, what? *I*
know! That's the effect she has on everybody. Well, I
leave you here, laddie. Oh, before we part – Butt! What
of Butt? Nature's worst blunder, don't you think?'

'I must say I've seen cheerier souls.'

'I think I've got him licked, Bertie. Charlotte is
coming to the Zoo with me this afternoon. Alone. And
later on to the pictures. That looks like the beginning
of the end, what? Well, toodle-oo, friend of my youth.
If you've nothing better to do this morning, you might
take a stroll along Bond Street and be picking out a
wedding present.'

I lost sight of Bingo after that. I left messages a couple
of times at the club, asking him to ring me up, but they
didn't have any effect. I took it that he was too busy
to respond. The Sons of the Red Dawn also passed out

of my life, though Jeeves told me he had met Comrade Butt one evening and had a brief chat with him. He reported Butt as gloomier than ever. In the competition for the bulging Charlotte, Butt had apparently gone right back in the betting.

'Mr Little would appear to have eclipsed him entirely, sir,' said Jeeves.

'Bad news, Jeeves; bad news!'

'Yes, sir.'

'I suppose what it amounts to, Jeeves, is that, when young Bingo really takes his coat off and starts in, there is no power of God or man that can prevent him making a chump of himself.'

'It would seem so, sir,' said Jeeves.

Then Goodwood came along, and I dug out the best suit and popped down.

I never know, when I'm telling a story, whether to cut the thing down to plain facts or whether to drool on and shove in a lot of atmosphere, and all that. I mean, many a cove would no doubt edge into the final spasm of this narrative with a long description of Goodwood, featuring the blue sky, the rolling prospect, the joyous crowds of pickpockets, and the parties of the second part who were having their pockets picked, and – in a word, what not. But better give it a miss, I think. Even if I wanted to go into details about the bally meeting I don't think I'd have the heart to. The thing's too recent. The anguish hasn't had time to pass. You see, what happened was that Ocean Breeze (curse him!) finished absolutely nowhere for the Cup. Believe me, nowhere.

These are the times that try men's souls. It's never pleasant to be caught in the machinery when a favourite comes unstitched, and in the case of this particular dashed animal, one had come to look on the running of the race as a pure formality, a sort of quaint, old-world ceremony to be gone through before one sauntered up to the bookie and collected. I had wandered out of the paddock to try and forget, when I bumped into old Bittlesham: and he looked so rattled and purple, and his eyes were standing out of his head at such an angle, that I simply pushed my hand out and shook his in silence.

'Me, too,' I said. 'Me, too. How much did *you* drop?'

'Drop?'

'On Ocean Breeze.'

'I did not bet on Ocean Breeze.'

'What! You owned the favourite for the Cup, and didn't back it!'

'I never bet on horse-racing. It is against my principles. I am told that the animal failed to win the contest.'

'Failed to win! Why, he was so far behind that he nearly came in first in the next race.'

'Tut!' said old Bittlesham.

'Tut is right,' I agreed. Then the rumminess of the thing struck me. 'But if you haven't dropped a parcel over the race,' I said, 'why are you looking so rattled?'

'That fellow is here!'

'What fellow?'

'That bearded man.'

It will show you to what an extent the iron had entered into my soul when I say that this was the first time I had given a thought to young Bingo. I suddenly remembered now that he had told me he would be at Goodwood.

'He is making an inflammatory speech at this very moment, specifically directed at me. Come! Where that crowd is.' He lugged me along and, by using his weight scientifically, got us into the front rank. 'Look! Listen!'

Young Bingo was certainly tearing off some ripe stuff. Inspired by the agony of having put his little all on a stumer that hadn't finished in the first six, he was fairly letting himself go on the subject of the blackness of the hearts of plutocratic owners who allowed a trusting public to imagine a horse was the real goods when it couldn't trot the length of its stable without getting its legs crossed and sitting down to rest. He then went on to draw what I'm bound to say was a most moving picture of a working man's home, due to this dishonesty. He showed us the working man, all optimism and simple trust, believing every word he read in the papers about Ocean Breeze's form; depriving his wife and children of food in order to back the brute; going without beer so as to be able to cram an extra bob on; robbing the baby's money-box with a hatpin on the eve of the race; and finally getting let down with a thud. Dashed impressive it was. I could see old Rowbotham nodding his head gently, while poor old Butt glowered at the speaker with ill-concealed jealousy. The audience ate it.

'But what does Lord Bittlesham care,' shouted Bingo, 'if the poor working man loses his hard-earned savings? I tell you, friends and comrades, you may talk, and you may argue, and you may cheer, and you may pass resolutions, but what you need is Action! Action! The world won't be a fit place for honest men to live in till the blood of Lord Bittlesham and his kind flows down the gutters of Park Lane!'

Roars of approval from the populace, most of whom, I suppose, had had their little bit on blighted Ocean Breeze, and were feeling it deeply. Old Bittlesham bounded over to a large, sad policeman who was watching the proceedings, and appeared to be urging him to rally round. The policeman pulled at his moustache, and smiled gently, but that was as far as he seemed inclined to go; and old Bittlesham came back to me, puffing not a little.

'It's monstrous! The man definitely threatens my personal safety, and that policeman declines to interfere. Said it was just talk! Talk! It's monstrous!'

'Absolutely,' I said, but I can't say it seemed to cheer him up much.

Comrade Butt had taken the centre of the stage now. He had a voice like the Last Trump, and you could hear every word he said, but somehow he didn't seem to be clicking. I suppose the fact was he was too impersonal, if that's the word I want. After Bingo's speech the audience was in the mood for something a good deal snappier than just general remarks about the Cause. They had started to heckle the poor blighter pretty freely, when he stopped in the middle of a sentence, and I saw that he was staring at old Bittlesham.

The crowd thought he had dried up.

'Suck a lozenge,' shouted someone.

Comrade Butt pulled himself together with a jerk, and even from where I stood I could see the nasty gleam in his eye.

'Ah,' he yelled, 'you may mock, comrades; you may jeer and sneer; and you may scoff; but let me tell you that the movement is spreading every day and every hour. Yes, even amongst the so-called upper classes it's spreading. Perhaps you'll believe me when I tell you that here, today, on this very spot, we have in our little band one of our most earnest workers, the nephew of that very Lord Bittlesham whose name you were hooting but a moment ago.'

And before old Bingo had a notion of what was up, he had reached out a hand and grabbed the beard. It came off all in one piece, and, well as Bingo's speech had gone, it was simply nothing compared with the hit made by this bit of business. I heard old Bittlesham give one short, sharp snort of amazement at my side, and then any remarks he may have made were drowned in thunders of applause.

I'm bound to say that in this crisis young Bingo acted with a good deal of decision and character. To grab Comrade Butt by the neck and try to twist his head off was with him the work of a moment. But before he could get any results the sad policeman, brightening up like magic, had charged in, and the next minute he was shoving his way back through the crowd, with Bingo in his right hand and Comrade Butt in his left.

'Let me pass, sir, please,' he said, civilly, as he came up against old Bittlesham, who was blocking the gangway.

'Eh?' said old Bittlesham, still dazed.

At the sound of his voice young Bingo looked up quickly from under the shadow of the policeman's right hand, and as he did so all the stuffing seemed to go out of him with a rush. For an instant he drooped like a bally lily, and then shuffled brokenly on. His air was the air of a man who has got it in the neck properly.

Sometimes when Jeeves has brought in my morning tea and shoved it on the table beside my bed, he drifts silently from the room and leaves me to go to it: at other times he sort of shimmies respectfully in the middle of the carpet, and then I know that he wants a word or two. On the day after I had got back from Goodwood I was lying on my back, staring at the ceiling, when I noticed that he was still in my midst.

'Oh, hallo,' I said. 'Yes?'

'Mr Little called earlier in the morning, sir.'

'Oh, by Jove, what? Did he tell you about what happened?'

'Yes, sir. It was in connection with that that he wished to see you. He proposes to retire to the country and remain there for some little while.'

'Dashed sensible.'

'That was my opinion, also sir. There was, however, a slight financial difficulty to be overcome. I took the liberty of advancing him ten pounds on your behalf to meet current expenses. I trust that meets with your approval, sir?'

'Oh, of course. Take a tenner off the dressing-table.'

'Very good, sir.'

'Jeeves,' I said.

'Sir?'

'What beats me is how the dickens the thing happened. I mean, how did the chappie Butt ever get to know who he was?'

Jeeves coughed.

'There, sir, I fear I may have been somewhat to blame.'

'You? How?'

'I fear I may carelessly have disclosed Mr Little's identity to Mr Butt on the occasion when I had that conversation with him.'

I sat up.

'What?'

'Indeed, now that I recall the incident, sir, I distinctly remember saying that Mr Little's work for the Cause really seemed to me to deserve something in the nature of public recognition. I greatly regret having been the means of bringing about a temporary estrangement between Mr Little and his lordship. And I am afraid there is another aspect to the matter. I am also responsible for the breaking off of relations between Mr Little and the young lady who came to tea here.'

I sat up again. It's a rummy thing, but the silver lining had absolutely escaped my notice till then.

'Do you mean to say it's off?'

'Completely, sir. I gathered from Mr Little's remarks that his hopes in the direction may now be looked on as definitely quenched. If there were no other obstacle, the young lady's father, I am informed by Mr Little, now regards him as a spy and a deceiver.'

'Well, I'm dashed!'

'I appear inadvertently to have caused much trouble, sir.'

'Jeeves!' I said.

'Sir?'

'How much money is there on the dressing-table?'

'In addition the ten-pound note which you instructed me to take, sir, there are two five-pound notes, three one-pounds, a ten-shillings, two half-crowns, a florin, four shillings, a sixpence, and a halfpenny, sir.'

'Collar it all,' I said. 'You've earned it.'

=11=
THE GREAT SERMON
HANDICAP

After Goodwood's over, I generally find that I get a bit restless. I'm not much of a lad for the birds and the trees and the great open spaces as a rule, but there's no doubt that London's not at its best in August, and rather tends to give me the pip and make me think of popping down into the country till things have bucked up a trifle. London, about a couple of weeks after that spectacular finish of young Bingo's which I've just been telling you about, was empty and smelled of burning asphalt. All my pals were away, most of the theatres were shut, and they were taking up Piccadilly in large spadefuls.

It was most infernally hot. As I sat in the old flat one night trying to muster up energy enough to go to bed, I felt I couldn't stand it much longer; and when Jeeves came in with the tissue-restorers on a tray I put the thing to him squarely.

'Jeeves,' I said, wiping the brow and gasping like a stranded goldfish, 'it's beastly hot.'

'The weather *is* oppressive, sir.'

'Not all the soda, Jeeves.'

'No, sir.'

'I think we've had about enough of the metrop. for the time being, and require a change. Shift-ho, I think, Jeeves, what?'

'Just as you say, sir. There is a letter on the tray, sir.'

'By Jove, Jeeves, that was practically poetry. Rhymed, did you notice?' I opened the letter. 'I say, this is rather extraordinary.'

'Sir?'

'You know Twing Hall?'

'Yes, sir.'

'Well, Mr Little is there.'

'Indeed, sir?'

'Absolutely in the flesh. He's had to take another of those tutoring jobs.'

After that fearful mix-up at Goodwood, when young Bingo Little, a broken man, had touched me for a tenner and whizzed silently off into the unknown, I had been all over the place, asking mutual friends if they had heard anything of him, but nobody had. And all the time he had been at Twing Hall. Rummy. And I'll tell you why it was rummy. Twing Hall belongs to old Lord Wickhammersley, a great pal of my guv'nor's when he was alive, and I have a standing invitation to pop down there when I like. I generally put in a week or two some time in the summer, and I was thinking of going there before I read the letter.

'And, what's more, Jeeves, my cousin Claude, and my cousin Eustace – you remember them?'

'Very vividly, sir.'

'Well, they're down there, too, reading for some exam. or other with the vicar. I used to read with him myself at one time. He's known far and wide as a pretty hot coach for those of fairly feeble intellect. Well, when I tell you he got *me* through Smalls, you'll gather that he's a bit of a hummer. I call this most extraordinary.'

I read the letter again. It was from Eustace. Claude and Eustace are twins, and more or less generally admitted to be the curse of the human race.

The Vicarage,
Twing, Glos.

Dear Bertie – Do you want to make a bit of money? I hear you had a bad Goodwood, so you probably do. Well, come down here quick and get in on the biggest sporting event of the season. I'll explain when I see you, but you can take it from me it's all right.

Claude and I are with a reading-party at old Heppenstall's. There are nine of us, not counting your pal Bingo Little, who is tutoring the kid up at the Hall.

Don't miss this golden opportunity, which may never occur again. Come and join us.

Yours,
Eustace.

I handed this to Jeeves. He studied it thoughtfully.

'What do you make of it? A rummy communication, what?'

'Very high-spirited young gentlemen, sir, Mr Claude and Mr Eustace. Up to some game, I should be disposed to imagine.'

'Yes. But what game, do you think?'

'It is impossible to say, sir. Did you observe that the letter continues over the page?'

'Eh, what?' I grabbed the thing. This was what was on the other side of the last page:

SERMON HANDICAP
RUNNERS AND BETTING
PROBABLE STARTERS

Rev. Joseph Tucker (Badgwick), scratch.
Rev. Leonard Starkie (Stapleton), scratch.

Rev. Alexander Jones (Upper Bingley), receives three minutes.

Rev. W. Dix (Little Clickton-in-the-Wold), receives five minutes.

Rev. Francis Heppenstall (Twing), receives eight minutes.

Rev. Cuthbert Dibble (Boustead Parva), receives nine minutes.

Rev. Orlo Hough (Boustead Magna), receives nine minutes.

Rev. J. J. Roberts (Fale-by-the-Water), receives ten minutes.

Rev. G. Hayward (Lower Bingley), receives twelve minutes.

Rev. James Bates (Gandle-by-the-Hill), receives fifteen minutes.

(The above have arrived.)

PRICES. – 5–2, Tucker, Starkie; 3–1, Jones; 9–2, Dix; 6–1, Heppenstall, Dibble, Hough; 100–8 any other.

It baffled me.

'Do you understand it, Jeeves?'

'No, sir.'

'Well, I think we ought to have a look into it, anyway, what?'

'Undoubtedly, sir.'

'Right-oh, then. Pack our spare dickey and a toothbrush in a neat brown-paper parcel, send a wire to Lord Wickhammersley to say we're coming, and buy two tickets on the five-ten at Paddington tomorrow.'

The five-ten was late as usual, and everybody was dressing for dinner when I arrived at the Hall. It was only by getting into my evening things in record time and taking the stairs to the dining-room in a couple of bounds that I managed to dead-heat with the soup. I slid into the vacant chair, and found that I was sitting next to old Wickhammersley's youngest daughter, Cynthia.

'Oh, hallo, old thing.' I said.

Great pals we've always been. In fact, there was a time when I had an idea I was in love with Cynthia. However, it blew over. A dashed pretty and lively and attractive girl, mind you, but full of ideals and all that. I may be wronging her, but I have an idea that she's the sort of girl who would want a fellow to carve out a career and what not. I know I've heard her speak favourably of Napoleon. So what with one thing and another the jolly old frenzy sort of petered out, and now we're just pals. I think she's a topper, and she thinks me next door to a looney, so everything's nice and matey.

'Well, Bertie, so you've arrived?'

'Oh, yes, I've arrived. Yes, here I am. I say, I seem to have plunged into the middle of quite a young dinner-party. Who are all these coves?'

'Oh, just people from round about. You know most of them. You remember Colonel Willis, and the Spencers – '

'Of course, yes. And there's old Heppenstall. Who's the other clergyman next to Mrs Spencer?'

'Mr. Hayward, from Lower Bingley.'

'What an amazing lot of clergymen there are round here. Why, there's another, next to Mrs Willis.'

'That's Mr Bates, Mr Heppenstall's nephew. He's an assistant-master at Eton. He's down here during the summer holidays, acting as locum tenens for Mr Spettigue, the rector of Gandle-by-the-Hill.'

'I thought I knew his face. He was in his fourth year

at Oxford when I was a fresher. Rather a blood. Got his rowing-blue and all that.' I took another look round the table, and spotted young Bingo. 'Ah, there he is,' I said. 'There's the old egg.'

'There's who?'

'Young Bingo Little. Great pal of mine. He's tutoring your brother, you know.'

'Good gracious! Is he a friend of yours?'

'Rather! Known him all my life.'

'Then tell me, Bertie, is he at all weak in the head?'

'Weak in the head?'

'I don't mean simply because he's a friend of yours. But he's so strange in his manner.'

'How do you mean?'

'Well, he keeps looking at me so oddly.'

'Oddly? How? Give me an imitation.'

'I can't in front of all these people.'

'Yes, you can. I'll hold my napkin up.'

'All right, then. Quick. There!'

Considering that she had only about a second and a half to do it in, I must say it was a jolly fine exhibition. She opened her mouth and eyes pretty wide and let her jaw drop sideways, and managed to look so like a dyspeptic calf and I recognized the symptoms immediately.

'Oh, that's all right,' I said. 'No need to be alarmed. He's simply in love with you.'

'In love with me. Don't be absurd.'

'My dear old thing, you don't know young Bingo. He can fall in love with *anybody*.'

'Thank you!'

'Oh, I didn't mean it that way, you know. I don't wonder at his taking to you. Why, I was in love with you myself once.'

'Once? Ah! And all that remains now are the cold ashes? This isn't one of your tactful evenings, Bertie.'

'Well, my dear sweet thing, dash it all, considering that you gave me the bird and nearly laughed yourself into a permanent state of hiccoughs when I asked you – '

'Oh, I'm not reproaching you. No doubt there were faults on both sides. He's very good-looking, isn't he?'

'Good-looking? Bingo? Bingo good-looking? No, I say, come now, really!'

'I mean, compared with some people,' said Cynthia.

Some time after this, Lady Wickhammersley gave the signal for the females of the species to leg it, and they duly stampeded. I didn't get a chance of talking to young Bingo when they'd gone, and later, in the drawing-room, he didn't show up. I found him eventually in his room, lying on the bed with his feet on the rail, smoking a toofah. There was a note-book on the counterpane beside him.

'Hallo, old scream,' I said.

'Hallo, Bertie,' he replied, in what seemed to me rather a moody, distrait sort of manner.

'Rummy finding you down here. I take it your uncle cut off your allowance after that Goodwood binge and you had to take this tutoring job to keep the wolf from the door?'

'Correct,' said young Bingo tersely.

'Well, you might have let your pals know where you were.'

He frowned darkly.

'I didn't want them to know where I was. I wanted to creep away and hide myself. I've been through a bad time, Bertie, these last weeks. The sun ceased to shine – '

'That's curious. We've had gorgeous weather in London.'

'The birds ceased to sing – '

'What birds?'

'What the devil does it matter what birds?' said young Bingo, with some asperity. 'Any birds. The birds round about here. You don't expect me to specify them by their pet names, do you? I tell you, Bertie, it hit me hard at first, very hard.'

'What hit you?' I simply couldn't follow the blighter.

'Charlotte's calculated callousness.'

'Oh, ah!' I've seen poor old Bingo through so many unsuccessful love-affairs that I'd almost forgotten there was a girl mixed up with that Goodwood business. Of course! Charlotte Corday Rowbotham. And she had given him the raspberry, I remembered, and gone off with Comrade Butt.

'I went through torments. Recently, however, I've – er – bucked up a bit. Tell me, Bertie, what are you doing down here? I didn't know you knew these people.'

'Me? Why, I've known them since I was a kid.'

Young Bingo put his feet down with a thud.

'Do you mean to say you've known Lady Cynthia all that time?'

'Rather! She can't have been seven when I met her first.'

'Good Lord!' said young Bingo. He looked at me for the first time as though I amounted to something, and swallowed a mouthful of smoke the wrong way. 'I love that girl, Bertie,' he went on, when he'd finished coughing.

'Yes. Nice girl, of course.'

He eyed me with pretty deep loathing.

'Don't speak of her in that horrible casual way. She's

an angel. An angel! Was she talking about me at all at dinner, Bertie?'

'Oh, yes.'

'What did she say?'

'I remember one thing. She said she thought you good-looking.'

Young Bingo closed his eyes in a sort of ecstasy. Then he picked up the note-book.

'Pop off now, old man, there's a good chap,' he said, in a hushed, far-away voice. 'I've got a bit of writing to do.'

'Writing?'

'Poetry, if you must know. I wish the dickens,' said young Bingo, not without some bitterness, 'she had been christened something except Cynthia. There isn't a dam' word in the language it rhymes with. Ye gods, how I could have spread myself if she had only been called Jane!'

Bright and early next morning, as I lay in bed blinking at the sunlight on the dressing-table and wondering when Jeeves was going to show up with a cup of tea, a heavy weight descended on my toes, and the voice of young Bingo polluted the air. The blighter had apparently risen with the lark.

'Leave me,' I said, 'I would be alone. I can't see anybody till I've had my tea.'

'When Cynthia smiles,' said young Bingo, 'the skies are blue; the world takes on a roseate hue; birds in the garden trill and sing, and Joy is king of everything, when Cynthia smiles.' He coughed, changing gears. 'When Cynthia frowns – '

'What the devil are you talking about?'

'I'm reading you my poem. The one I wrote to Cynthia last night. I'll go on, shall I?'

'No!'

'No?'

'No. I haven't had my tea.'

At this moment Jeeves came in with the good old beverage, and I sprang on it with a glad cry. After a couple of sips things looked a bit brighter. Even young Bingo didn't offend the eye to quite such an extent. By the time I'd finished the first cup I was a new man, so much so that I not only permitted but encouraged the poor fish to read the rest of the bally thing, and even went so far as to criticize the scansion of the fourth line of the fifth verse. We were still arguing the point when the door burst open and in blew Claude and Eustace. One of the things which discourages me about rural life is the frightful earliness with which events begin to break loose. I've stayed at places in the country where they've jerked me out of the dreamless at about six-thirty to go for a jolly swim in the lake. At Twing, thank heaven, they know me, and let me breakfast in bed.

The twins seemed pleased to see me.

'Good old Bertie!' said Claude.

'Stout fellow!' said Eustace. 'The Rev. told us you had arrived. I thought that letter of mine would fetch you.'

'You can always bank on Bertie,' said Claude. 'A sportsman to the finger-tips. Well, has Bingo told you about it?'

'Not a word. He's been – '

'We've been talking,' said Bingo hastily, 'of other matters.'

Claude pinched the last slice of thin bread-and-butter, and Eustace poured himself out a cup of tea.

'It's like this, Bertie,' said Eustace, settling down cosily. 'As I told you in my letter, there are nine of us marooned in this desert spot, reading with old Heppen-stall. Well, of course, nothing is jollier than sweating up the Classics when it's a hundred in the shade, but there does come a time when you begin to feel the need of a little relaxation; and, by Jove, there are absolutely no facilities for relaxation in this place whatever. And then Steggles got this idea. Steggles is one of our read-ing-party, and, between ourselves, rather a worm as a general thing. Still, you have to give him credit for getting this idea.'

'What idea?'

'Well, you know how many parsons there are round about here. There are about a dozen hamlets within a radius of six miles, and each hamlet has a church and each church has a parson and each parson preaches a sermon every Sunday. Tomorrow week – Sunday the twenty-third – we're running off the great Sermon Handicap. Steggles is making the book. Each parson is to be clocked by a reliable steward of the course, and the one that preaches the longest sermon wins. Did you study the race-card I sent you?'

'I couldn't understand what it was all about.'

'Why, you chump, it gives the handicaps and the current odds on each starter. I've got another one here, in case you've lost yours. Take a careful look at it. It gives you the thing in a nutshell. Jeeves, old son, do you want a sporting flutter?'

'Sir?' said Jeeves, who had just meandered in with my breakfast.

Claude explained the scheme. Amazing the way Jeeves grasped it right off. But he merely smiled in a paternal sort of way.

'Thank you, sir, I think not.'

'Well, you're with us, Bertie, aren't you?' said Claude, sneaking a roll and a slice of bacon. 'Have you studied that card? Well, tell me, does anything strike you about it?'

Of course it did. It had struck me the moment I looked at it.

'Why, it's a sitter for old Heppenstall,' I said. 'He's got the event sewed up in a parcel. There isn't a parson in the land who could give him eight minutes. Your pal Steggles must be an ass, giving him a handicap like that. Why, in the days when I was with him, old Heppenstall never used to preach under half an hour, and there was one sermon of his on Brotherly Love which lasted forty-five minutes if it lasted a second. Has he lost his vim lately, or what is it?'

'Not a bit of it,' said Eustace. 'Tell him what happened, Claude.'

'Why,' said Claude, 'the first Sunday we were here, we all went to Twing church, and old Heppenstall preached a sermon that was well under twenty minutes. This is what happened. Steggles didn't notice it, and the Rev. didn't notice it himself, but Eustace and I both spotted that he had dropped a chunk of at least half a dozen pages out of his sermon-case as he was walking up to the pulpit. He sort of flickered when he got to the gap in the manuscript, but carried on all right, and Steggles went away with the impression that twenty minutes or a bit under was his usual form. The next Sunday we heard Tucker and Starkie, and they both went well over thirty-five minutes, so Steggles arranged the handicapping as you see on the card. You must come into this, Bertie. You see, the trouble is that I haven't a bean, and Eustace hasn't a bean, and Bingo Little hasn't a bean, so you'll have to finance the syndicate. Don't weaken! It's just putting money in all our pockets. Well, we'll have to be getting back now. Think the thing over, and phone me later in the day. And, if you let us down, Bertie, may a cousin's curse – Come on, Claude, old thing.'

The more I studied the scheme, the better it looked.

'How about it, Jeeves?' I said.

Jeeves smiled gently, and drifted out.

'Jeeves has no sporting blood,' said Bingo.

'Well, I have. I'm coming into this. Claude's quite right. It's like finding money by the wayside.'

'Good man!' said Bingo. 'Now I can see daylight. Say I have a tenner on Heppenstall, and cop; that'll give me a bit in hand to back Pink Pill with in the two o'clock at Gatwick the week after next: cop on that, put the pile on Musk-Rat for the one-thirty at Lewes, and there I am with a nice little sum to take to Alexandra Park on September the tenth, when I've got a tip straight from the stable.'

It sounded like a bit out of "Smiles's Self-Help".

'And then,' said young Bingo, 'I'll be in a position to go to my uncle and beard him in his lair somewhat. He's quite a bit of a snob, you know, and when he hears that I'm going to marry the daughter of an earl – '

'I say, old man,' I couldn't help saying, 'aren't you looking ahead rather far?'

'Oh, that's all right. It's true nothing's actually settled yet, but she practically told me the other day she was fond of me.'

'What!'

'Well, she said that the sort of man she liked was the self-reliant, manly man with strength, good looks, character, ambition, and initiative.'

'Leave me, laddie,' I said. 'Leave me to my fried egg.'

Directly I'd got up I went to the phone, snatched Eustace away from his morning's work, and instructed him to put a tenner on the Twing flier at current odds for each of the syndicate; and after lunch Eustace rang me up to say that he had done business at a snappy seven-to-one, the odds having lengthened owing to a rumour in knowledgeable circles that the Rev. was subject to hayfever, and was taking big chances strolling in the paddock behind the Vicarage in the early mornings. And it was dashed lucky, I thought next day, that we had managed to get the money on in time, for on the Sunday morning old Heppenstall fairly took the bit between his teeth, and gave us thirty-six solid minutes on Certain Popular Superstitions. I was sitting next to Steggles in the pew, and I saw him blench visibly. He was a little rat-faced fellow, with shifty eyes and a suspicious nature. The first thing he did when we emerged into the open air was to announce, formally, that anyone who fancied the Rev. could now be accommodated at fifteen-to-eight on, and he added, in a rather nasty manner, that if he had his way, this sort of in-and-out running would be brought to the attention of the Jockey Club, but that he supposed that there was nothing to be done about it. This ruinous price checked the punters at once, and there was little money in sight. And so matters stood till just after lunch on Tuesday afternoon, when, as I was strolling up and down in front of the house with a cigarette, Claude and Eustace came bursting up the drive on bicycles, dripping with momentous news.

'Bertie,' said Claude, deeply agitated, 'unless we take immediate action and do a bit of quick thinking, we're in the cart.'

'What's the matter?'

'G. Hayward's the matter,' said Eustace morosely. 'The Lower Bingley starter.'

'We never even considered him,' said Claude. 'Somehow or other, he got overlooked. It's always the way. Steggles overlooked him. We all overlooked him. But Eustace and I happened by the merest fluke to be riding through Lower Bingley this morning, and there was a wedding on at the church, and it suddenly struck us that it wouldn't be a bad move to get a line on G. Hayward's form, in case he might be a dark horse.'

'And it was jolly lucky we did,' said Eustace. 'He delivered an address of twenty-six minutes by Claude's stop-watch. At a village wedding, mark you! What'll he do when he really extends himself!'

'There's only one thing to be done, Bertie,' said Claude. 'You must spring some more funds, so that we can hedge on Hayward and save ourselves.'

'But – '

'Well, it's the only way out.'

'But I say, you know, I hate the idea of all that money we put on Heppenstall being chucked away.'

'What else can you suggest? You don't suppose the Rev. can give this absolute marvel a handicap and win, do you?'

'I've got it!' I said.

'What?'

'I see a way by which we can make it safe for our nominee. I'll pop over this afternoon, and ask him as a personal favour to preach that sermon of his on Brotherly Love on Sunday.'

Claude and Eustace looked at each other, like those chappies in the poem, with a wild surmise.

'It's a scheme,' said Claude.

'A jolly brainy scheme,' said Eustace. 'I didn't think you had it in you, Bertie.'

'But even so,' said Claude, 'fizzer as that sermon no doubt is, will it be good enough in the face of a four-minute handicap?'

'Rather!' I said. 'When I told you it lasted forty-five minutes, I was probably understating it. I should call it – from my recollection of the thing – nearer fifty.'

'Then carry on,' said Claude.

I toddled over in the evening and fixed the thing up. Old Heppenstall was most decent about the whole affair. He seemed pleased and touched that I should have remembered the sermon all these years, and said he had once or twice had an idea of preaching it again, only it had seemed to him, on reflection, that it was perhaps a trifle long for a rustic congregation.

'And in these restless times, my dear Wooster,' he said, 'I fear that brevity in the pulpit is becoming more and more desiderated by even the bucolic churchgoer, who one might have supposed would be less afflicted with the spirit of hurry and impatience than his metropolitan brother. I have had many arguments on the subject with my nephew, young Bates, who is taking my old friend Spettigue's cure over at Gandle-by-the-Hill. His view is that a sermon nowadays should be a bright, brisk, straight-from-the-shoulder address, never lasting more than ten or twelve minutes.'

'Long?' I said. 'Why, my goodness! you don't call that Brotherly Love sermon of yours *long*, do you?'

'It takes fully fifty minutes to deliver.'

'Surely not?'

'Your incredulity, my dear Wooster, is extremely flattering – far more flattering, of course, than I deserve. Nevertheless, the facts are as I have stated. You are sure that I would not be well advised to make certain excisions and eliminations? You do not think it would be a good thing to cut, to prune? I might, for example, delete the rather exhaustive excursus into the family life of the early Assyrians?'

'Don't touch a word of it, or you'll spoil the whole thing,' I said earnestly.

'I am delighted to hear you say so, and I shall preach the sermon without fail next Sunday morning.'

What I have always said, and what I always shall say, is, that this ante-post betting is a mistake, an error, and a mug's game. You never can tell what's going to happen. If fellows would only stick to the good old S.P. there would be fewer young men go wrong. I'd hardly finished my breakfast on the Saturday morning, when Jeeves came to my bedside to say that Eustace wanted me on the telephone.

'Good Lord, Jeeves, what's the matter, do you think?'

I'm bound to say I was beginning to get a bit jumpy by this time.

'Mr Eustace did not confide in me, sir.'

'Has he got the wind up?'

'Somewhat vertically, sir, to judge by his voice.'

'Do you know what I think, Jeeves? Something's gone wrong with the favourite.'

'Which is the favourite, sir?'

'Mr Heppenstall. He's gone to odds on. He was intending to preach a sermon on Brotherly Love which would have brought him home by lengths. I wonder if anything's happened to him.'

'You could ascertain, sir, by speaking to Mr Eustace on the telephone. He is holding the wire.'

'By Jove, yes!'

I shoved on a dressing-gown, and flew downstairs like a mighty, rushing wind. The moment I heard Eustace's voice I knew we were for it. It had a croak of agony in it.

'Bertie?'

'Here I am.'

'Deuce of a time you've been. Bertie, we're sunk. The favourite's blown up.'

'No!'

'Yes. Coughing in his stable all last night.'

'What!'

'Absolutely! Hay-fever.'

'Oh, my sainted aunt!'

'The doctor is with him now, and it's only a question of minutes before he's officially scratched. That means the curate will show up at the post instead, and he's no good at all. He is being offered at a hundred-to-six, but no takers. What shall we do?'

I had a grapple with the thing for a moment in silence.

'Eustace.'

'Hallo?'

'What can you get on G. Hayward?'

'Only four to one now. I think there's been a leak, and Steggles has heard something. The odds shortened late last night in a significant manner.'

'Well, four to one will clear us. Put another fiver all round on G. Hayward for the syndicate. That'll bring us out on the right side of the ledger.'

'If he wins.'

'What do you mean? I thought you considered him a cert., bar Heppenstall.'

'I'm beginning to wonder,' said Eustace gloomily, 'if there's such a thing as a cert., in this world. I'm told the Rev. Joseph Tucker did an extraordinarily fine trial gallop at a mothers' meeting over at Badgwick yesterday. However, it seems our only chance. So-long.'

Not being one of the official stewards, I had my choice of churches next morning, and naturally I didn't hesitate. The only drawback to going to Lower Bingley was that it was ten miles away, which meant an early start, but I borrowed a bicycle from one of the grooms and tooled off. I had only Eustace's word for it that G. Hayward was such a stayer, and it might have been that he had showed too flattering form at that wedding where the twins had heard him preach; but any misgivings I may have had disappeared the moment he got into the pulpit. Eustace had been right. The man was a trier. He was a tall, rangy-looking greybeard, and he went off from the start with a nice, easy action, pausing and clearing his throat at the end of each sentence, and it wasn't five minutes before I realized that here was the winner. His habit of stopping dead and looking round the church at intervals was worth minutes to us, and in the home stretch we gained no little advantage owing to his dropping his pince-nez and having to grope for them. At the twenty-minute mark he had merely settled down. Twenty-five minutes saw him going strong. And when he finally finished with a good burst, the clock showed thirty-five minutes fourteen seconds. With the handicap which he had been given, this seemed to me to make the event easy for him, and it was with much *bonhomie* and goodwill to all men that I hopped on to the old bike and started back to the Hall for lunch.

Bingo was talking on the 'phone when I arrived.

'Fine! Splendid! Topping!' he was saying. 'Eh? Oh, we needn't worry about him. Right-o, I'll tell Bertie.' He hung up the receiver and caught sight of me. Oh, hallo, Bertie; I was just talking to Eustace. It's all right, old man. The report from Lower Bingley has just got in. G. Hayward romps home.'

'I knew he would. I've just come from there.'

'Oh, were you there? I went to Badgwick. Tucker ran a splendid race, but the handicap was too much for him. Starkie had a sore throat and was nowhere. Roberts, of Fale-by-the-Water, ran third. Good old G. Hayward!'

said Bingo affectionately, and we strolled out on to the terrace.

'Are all the returns in, then?' I asked.

'All except Gandle-by-the-Hill. But we needn't worry about Bates. He never had a chance. By the way, poor old Jeeves loses his tenner. Silly ass!'

'Jeeves? How do you mean?'

'He came to me this morning, just after you had left, and asked me to put a tenner on Bates for him. I told him he was a chump, and begged him not to throw his money away, but he would do it.'

'I beg your pardon, sir. This note arrived for you just after you had left the house this morning.'

Jeeves had materialized from nowhere, and was standing at my elbow.

'Eh? What? Note?'

'The Reverend Mr Heppenstall's butler brought it over from the Vicarage, sir. It came too late to be delivered to you at the moment.'

Young Bingo was talking to Jeeves like a father on the subject of betting against the form-book. The yell I gave made him bite his tongue in the middle of a sentence.

'What the dickens is the matter?' he asked, not a little peeved.

'We're dished! Listen to this!'

I read him the note:

> The Vicarage,
> Twing, Glos.
>
> My Dear Wooster – As you may have heard, circumstances over which I have no control will prevent my preaching the sermon on Brotherly Love for which you made such a flattering request. I am unwilling, however, that you shall be disappointed, so, if you

will attend divine service at Gandle-by-the-Hill this morning, you will hear my sermon preached by young Bates, my nephew. I have lent him the manuscript at his urgent desire, for, between ourselves, there are wheels within wheels. My nephew is one of the candidates for the headmastership of a well-known public school, and the choice has narrowed down between him and one rival.

Late yesterday evening James received private information that the head of the Board of Governors of the school proposed to sit under him this Sunday in order to judge of the merits of his preaching, a most important item in swaying the Board's choice. I acceded to his plea that I lend him my sermon on Brotherly Love, of which, like you, he apparently retains a vivid recollection. It would have been too late for him to compose a sermon of suitable length in place of the brief address which – mistakenly, in my opinion, – he had designed to deliver to his rustic flock, and I wished to help the boy.

Trusting that his preaching of the sermon will supply you with as pleasant memories as you say you have of mine, I remain,

Cordially yours,
F. Heppenstall.

P.S. – The hay-fever has rendered my eyes unpleasantly weak for the time being, so I am dictating this letter to my butler, Brookfield, who will convey it to you.

I don't know when I've experienced a more massive silence than the one that followed my reading of this cheery epistle. Young Bingo gulped once or twice, and practically every known emotion came and went on his face. Jeeves coughed one soft, low, gentle cough like a sheep with a blade of grass stuck in its throat, and then stood gazing serenely at the landscape. Finally young Bingo spoke.

'Great Scott!' he whispered hoarsely. 'An S.P. job!'

'I believe that is the technical term, sir,' said Jeeves.

'So you had inside information, dash it!' said young Bingo.

'Why, yes, sir,' said Jeeves. 'Brookfield happened to mention the contents of the note to me when he brought it. We are old friends.'

Bingo registered grief, anguish, rage, despair and resentment.

'Well, all I can say,' he cried, 'is that it's a bit thick! Preaching another man's sermon! Do you call that honest? Do you call that playing the game?'

'Well, my dear old thing,' I said, 'be fair. It's quite within the rules. Clergymen do it all the time. They aren't expected always to make up the sermons they preach.'

Jeeves coughed again, and fixed me with an expressionless eye.

'And in the present case, sir, if I may be permitted to take the liberty of making the observation, I think we should make allowances. We should remember that the securing of this headmastership meant everything to the young couple.'

'Young couple? What young couple?'

'The Reverend James Bates, sir, and Lady Cynthia. I am informed by her ladyship's maid that they have been engaged to be married for some weeks – provisionally, so to speak; and his lordship made his consent conditional on Mr Bates securing a really important and remunerative position.'

Young Bingo turned a light green.

'Engaged to be married!'

'Yes, sir.'

There was a silence.

'I think I'll go for a walk,' said Bingo.

'But, my dear old thing,' I said, 'it's just lunch-time. The gong will be going any minute now.'

'I don't want any lunch!' said Bingo.

=12=
THE PURITY OF THE TURF

After that, life at Twing jogged along pretty peacefully
for a bit. Twing is one of those places where there isn't
a frightful lot to do nor any very hectic excitement to
look forward to. In fact, the only event of any import-
ance on the horizon, as far as I could ascertain, was the
annual village school treat. One simply filled in the time
by loafing about the grounds, playing a bit of tennis,
and avoiding young Bingo as far as was humanly
possible.

This last was a very necessary move if you wanted a
happy life, for the Cynthia affair had jarred the unfortunate mutt to such an extent that he was always waylaying one and decanting his anguished soul. And when,
one morning, he blew into my bedroom while I was
toying with a bit of breakfast, I decided to take a firm
line from the start. I could stand having him moaning
all over me after dinner, and even after lunch; but at
breakfast, no. We Woosters are amiability itself, but
there is a limit.

'Now look here, old friend,' I said. 'I know your bally
heart is broken and all that, and at some future time I
shall be delighted to hear all about it, but – '

'I didn't come to talk about that.'

'No? Good egg!'

'The past,' said young Bingo, 'is dead. Let us say no
more about it.'

'Right-o!'

'I have been wounded to the very depths of my soul, but don't speak about it.'

'I won't.'

'Ignore it. Forget it.'

'Absolutely!'

I hadn't seen him so dashed reasonable for days.

'What I came to see you about this morning, Bertie,' he said, fishing a sheet of paper out of his pocket, 'was to ask if you would care to come in on another little flutter.'

If there is one thing we Woosters are simply dripping with, it is sporting blood. I bolted the rest of my sausage, and sat up and took notice.

'Proceed,' I said. 'You interest me strangely, old bird.'

Bingo laid the paper on the bed.

'On Monday week,' he said, 'you may or may not know, the annual village school treat takes place. Lord Wickhammersley lends the Hall grounds for the purpose. There will be games, and a conjurer, and coconut shies, and tea in a tent. And also sports.'

'I know. Cynthia was telling me.'

Young Bingo winced.

'Would you mind not mentioning that name? I am not made of marble.'

'Sorry!'

'Well, as I was saying, this jamboree is slated for Monday week. The question is, Are we on?'

'How do you mean, "Are we on?"?'

'I am referring to the sports. Steggles did so well out of the Sermon Handicap that he has decided to make a book on these sports. Punters can be accommodated at ante-post odds or starting price, according to their preference. I think we ought to look into it,' said young Bingo.

I pressed the bell.

'I'll consult Jeeves. I don't touch any sporting proposition without his advice. Jeeves,' I said, as he drifted in, 'rally round.'

'Sir?'

'Stand by. We want your advice.'

'Very good, sir.'

'State your case, Bingo.'

Bingo stated his case.

'What about it, Jeeves?' I said. 'Do we go in?'

Jeeves pondered to some extent.

'I am inclined to favour the idea, sir.'

That was good enough for me. 'Right,' I said. 'Then we will form a syndicate and bust the Ring. I supply the money, you supply the brains, and Bingo – what do you supply, Bingo?'

'If you will carry me, and let me settle up later,' said young Bingo, 'I think I can put you in the way of winning a parcel on the Mothers' Sack Race.'

'All right. We will put you down as Inside Information. Now, what are the events?'

Bingo reached for his paper and consulted it.

'Girls' Under Fourteen Fifty-Yard Dash seems to open the proceedings.'

'Anything to say about that, Jeeves?'

'No, sir. I have no information.'

'What's the next?'

'Boys' and Girls' Mixed Animal Potato Race, All Ages.'

This was a new one to me. I had never heard of it at any of the big meetings.

'What's that?'

'Rather sporting,' said young Bingo. 'The competitors enter in couples, each couple being assigned an animal cry and a potato. For instance, let's suppose that you

184

and Jeeves entered. Jeeves would stand at a fixed point holding a potato. You would have your head in a sack, and you would grope about trying to find Jeeves and making a noise like a cat; Jeeves also making a noise like a cat. Other competitors would be making noises like cows and pigs and dogs, and so on, and groping about for *their* potato-holders, who would also be making noises like cows and pigs and dogs and so on – '

I stopped the poor fish.

'Jolly if you're fond of animals,' I said, 'but on the whole – '

'Precisely, sir,' said Jeeves. 'I wouldn't touch it.'

'Too open, what?'

'Exactly, sir. Very hard to estimate form.'

'Carry on, Bingo. Where do we go from there?'

'Mothers' Sack Race.'

'Ah! that's better. This is where you know something.'

'A gift for Mrs Penworthy, the tobacconist's wife,' said Bingo confidently. 'I was in at her shop yesterday, buying cigarettes, and she told me she had won three times at fairs in Worcestershire. She only moved to these parts a short time ago, so nobody knows about her. She promised me she would keep herself dark, and I think we could get a good price.'

'Risk a tenner each way, Jeeves, what?'

'I think so, sir.'

'Girls' Open Egg and Spoon Race,' read Bingo.

'How about that?'

'I doubt if it would be worth while to invest, sir,' said Jeeves. 'I am told it is a certainty for last year's winner, Sarah Mills, who will doubtless start an odds-on favourite.'

'Good, is she?'

'They tell me in the village that she carries a beautiful egg, sir.'

'Then there's the Obstacle Race,' said Bingo. 'Risky, in my opinion. Like betting on the Grand National. Fathers' Hat-Trimming Contest — another speculative event. That's all, except for the Choir-Boys' Hundred Yards Handicap, for a pewter mug presented by the vicar — open to all whose voices have not broken before the second Sunday in Epiphany. Willie Chambers won last year, in a canter, receiving fifteen yards. This time he will probably be handicapped out of the race. I don't know what to advise.'

'If I might make a suggestion, sir.'

I eyed Jeeves with interest. I don't know that I'd ever seen him look so nearly excited.

'You've got something up your sleeve?'

'I have, sir.'

'Red-hot?'

'That precisely describes it, sir. I think I may confidently assert that we have the winner of the Choir-Boys' Handicap under this very roof, sir. Harold, the page-boy.'

'Page-boy? Do you mean the tubby little chap in buttons one sees bobbing about here and there? Why, dash it, Jeeves, nobody has a greater respect for your knowledge of form than I have, but I'm hanged if I can see Harold catching the judge's eye. He's practically circular, and every time I've seen him he's been leaning up against something, half asleep.'

'He receives thirty yards, sir, and could win from scratch. The boy is a flier.'

'How do you know?'

Jeeves coughed, and there was a dreamy look in his eye.

'I was as much astonished as yourself, sir, when I

first became aware of the lad's capabilities. I happened to pursue him one morning with the intention of fetching him a clip on the side of the head – '

'Great Scott, Jeeves! You?'

'Yes, sir. The boy is of an outspoken disposition, and had made an opprobrious remark respecting my personal appearance.'

'What did he say about your appearance?'

'I have forgotten, sir,' said Jeeves, with a touch of austerity. 'But it was opprobrious. I endeavoured to correct him, but he outdistanced me by yards and made good his escape.'

'But, I say, Jeeves, this is sensational. And yet – if he's such a sprinter, why hasn't anybody in the village found it out? Surely he plays with the other boys?'

'No, sir. As his lordship's page-boy, Harold does not mix with the village lads.'

'Bit of a snob, what?'

'He is somewhat acutely alive to the existence of class distinctions, sir.'

'You're absolutely certain he's such a wonder?' said Bingo. 'I mean, it wouldn't do to plunge unless you're sure.'

'If you desire to ascertain the boy's form by personal inspection, sir, it will be a simple matter to arrange a secret trial.'

'I'm bound to say I should feel easier in my mind,' I said.

'Then if I may take a shilling from the money on your dressing-table – '

'What for?'

'I propose to bribe the lad to speak slightingly of the second footman's squint, sir. Charles is somewhat sensitive on the point, and should undoubtedly make the lad extend himself. If you will be at the first-floor

187

passage-window, overlooking the back door, in half an hour's time – '

I don't know when I've dressed in such a hurry. As a rule, I'm what you might call a slow and careful dresser: I like to linger over the tie and see that the trousers are just so; but this morning I was all worked up. I just shoved on my things anyhow, and joined Bingo at the window with a quarter of an hour to spare.

The passage-window looked down on to a broad sort of paved courtyard, which ended after about twenty yards in an archway through a high wall. Beyond this archway you got on to a strip of the drive, which curved round for another thirty yards or so, till it was lost behind a thick shrubbery. I put myself in the stripling's place and thought what steps I would take with a second footman after me. There was only one thing to do – leg it for the shrubbery and take cover; which meant that at least fifty yards would have to be covered – an excellent test. If good old Harold could fight off the second footman's challenge long enough to allow him to reach the bushes, there wasn't a choir-boy in England who could give him thirty yards in the hundred. I waited, all of a twitter, for what seemed hours, and then suddenly there was a confused noise without, and something round and blue and buttony shot through the back door and buzzed for the archway like a mustang. And about two seconds later out came the second footman, going his hardest.

There was nothing to it. Absolutely nothing. The field never had a chance. Long before the footman reached the half-way mark, Harold was in the bushes, throwing stones. I came away from the window thrilled to the marrow; and when I met Jeeves on the stairs I was so moved that I nearly grasped his hand.

'Jeeves,' I said, 'no discussion! The Wooster shirt goes on this boy!'

'Very good, sir,' said Jeeves.

The worst of these country meetings is that you can't plunge as heavily as you would like when you get a good thing, because it alarms the Ring. Steggles, though pimpled, was, as I have indicated, no chump, and if I had invested all I wanted to he would have put two and two together. I managed to get a good solid bet down for the syndicate, however, though it did make him look thoughtful. I heard in the next few days that he had been making searching inquiries in the village concerning Harold; but nobody could tell him anything, and eventually he came to the conclusion, I suppose, that I must be having a long shot on the strength of that thirty-yards start. Public opinion wavered between Jimmy Goode, receiving ten yards, at seven-to-two, and Alexander Bartlett, with six yards start, at eleven-to-four. Willie Chambers, scratch, was offered to the public at two-to-one, but found no takers.

We were taking no chances on the big event, and directly we had got our money on at a nice hundred-to-twelve, Harold was put into strict training. It was a wearing business, and I can understand now why most of the big trainers are grim, silent men, who look as though they had suffered. The kid wanted constant watching. It was no good talking to him about honour and glory and how proud his mother would be when he wrote and told her he had won a real cup – the moment blighted Harold discovered that training meant knocking off pastry, taking exercise, and keeping away from the cigarettes, he was all against it, and it was only by unceasing vigilance that we managed to keep him in any shape at all. It was the diet that was the stumbling-block. As far as exercise went, we could generally arrange for a sharp dash every morning with the assistance of the second footman. It ran into money, of course, but that couldn't be helped. Still, when a kid has simply to wait till the butler's back is turned to have the run of the pantry, and has only to nip into the smoking-room to collect a handful of the best Turkish, training becomes a rocky job. We could only hope that on the day his natural stamina would pull him through.

And then one evening young Bingo came back from the links with a disturbing story. He had been in the habit of giving Harold mild exercise in the afternoons by taking him out as a caddie.

At first he seemed to think it humorous, the poor chump! He bubbled over with merry mirth as he began his tale.

'I say, rather funny this afternoon,' he said. 'You ought to have seen Steggles's face!'

'Seen Steggles's face? What for?'

'When he saw young Harold sprint, I mean.'

I was filled with a grim foreboding of an awful doom.

'Good heavens! You didn't let Harold sprint in front of Steggles?'

Young Bingo's jaw dropped.

'I never thought of that,' he said, gloomily. 'It wasn't my fault. I was playing a round with Steggles, and after we'd finished we went into the club-house for a drink, leaving Harold with the clubs outside. In about five minutes we came out, and there was the kid on the gravel practising swings with Steggles's driver and a stone. When he saw us coming, the kid dropped the club and was over the horizon like a streak. Steggles was absolutely dumbfounded. And I must say it was a revelation to me. The kid certainly gave of his best. Of course, it's a nuisance in a way; but I don't see, on second thoughts,' said Bingo, brightening up, 'what it matters. We're in at a good price. We've nothing to lose by the kid's form becoming known. I take it he will start odds-on, but that doesn't affect us.'

I looked at Jeeves. Jeeves looked at me.

'It affects us all right if he doesn't start at all.'

'Precisely, sir.'

'What do you mean?' asked Bingo.

'If you ask me,' I said, 'I think Steggles will try to nobble him before the race.'

'Good Lord! I never thought of that.' Bingo blenched. 'You don't think he would really do it?'

'I think he would have a jolly good try. Steggles is a bad man. From now on, Jeeves, we must watch Harold like hawks.'

'Undoubtedly, sir.'

'Ceaseless vigilance, what?'

'Precisely, sir.'

'You wouldn't care to sleep in his room, Jeeves?'

'No, sir, I should not.'

'No, nor would I, if it comes to that. But dash it all,' I said, 'we're letting ourselves get rattled! We're losing our nerve. This won't do. How can Steggles possibly get at Harold, even if he wants to?'

There was no cheering young Bingo up. He's one of those birds who simply leap at the morbid view, if you give them half a chance.

'There are all sorts of ways of nobbling favourites,' he said, in a sort of death-bed voice. 'You ought to read some of these racing novels. In "Pipped on the Post", Lord Jasper Maulevereras near as a toucher outed Bonny Betsy by bribing the head lad to slip a cobra into her stable the night before the Derby!'

'What are the chances of a cobra biting Harold, Jeeves?'

'Slight, I should imagine, sir. And in such an event, knowing the boy as intimately as I do, my anxiety would be entirely for the snake.'

'Still, unceasing vigilance, Jeeves.'

'Most certainly, sir.'

I must say I got a bit fed with young Bingo in the next few days. It's all very well for a fellow with a big winner in his stable to exercise proper care, but in my opinion Bingo overdid it. The blighter's mind appeared to be absolutely saturated with racing fiction; and in stories of that kind, as far as I could make out, no horse is ever allowed to start in a race without at least a dozen attempts to put it out of action. He stuck to Harold like a plaster. Never let the unfortunate kid out of his sight. Of course, it meant a lot to the poor old egg if he could collect on this race, because it would give him enough money to chuck his tutoring job and get back to London; but all the same, he needn't have woken me up at three in the morning twice running – once to tell me we ought to cook Harold's food ourselves to prevent doping: the other time to say that he had heard mysterious noises in the shrubbery. But he reached the limit, in my opinion, when he insisted on my going to evening service on Sunday, the day before the sports.

'Why on earth?' I said, never being much of a lad for even-song.

'Well, I can't go myself. I shan't be here. I've got to go to London today with young Egbert.' Egbert was Lord Wickhammersley's son, the one Bingo was tutoring. 'He's going for a visit down in Kent, and I've got to see him off at Charing Cross. It's an infernal nuisance. I shan't be back till Monday afternoon. In fact, I shall miss most of the sports, I expect. Everything, therefore, depends on you, Bertie.'

'But why should either of us go to evening service?'

'Ass! Harold sings in the choir, doesn't he?'

'What about it? I can't stop him dislocating his neck over a high note, if that's what you're afraid of.'

'Fool! Steggles sings in the choir, too. There may be dirty work after the service.'

'What absolute rot!'

'Is it?' said young Bingo. 'Well, let me tell you that in "Jenny, the Girl Jockey", the villain kidnapped the boy who was to ride the favourite the night before the big race, and he was the only one who understood and could control the horse, and if the heroine hadn't dressed up in riding things and – '

'Oh, all right, all right. But, if there's any danger, it seems to me the simplest thing would be for Harold not to turn out on Sunday evening.'

'He must turn out. You seem to think the infernal kid is a monument of rectitude, beloved by all. He's got the shakiest reputation of any kid in the village. His name is as near being mud as it can jolly well stick. He's played hookey from the choir so often that the vicar told him, if one more thing happened, he would fire him out. Nice chumps we should look if he was scratched the night before the race!'

Well, of course, that being so, there was nothing for it but to toddle along.

There's something about evening service in a country church that makes a fellow feel drowsy and peaceful. Sort of end-of-a-prefect-day feeling. Old Heppenstall was up in the pulpit, and he has a kind of regular, bleating delivery that assists thought. They had left the door open, and the air was full of a mixed scent of trees and honeysuckle and mildew and villagers' Sunday clothes. As far as the eye could reach, you could see farmers propped up in restful attitudes, breathing heavily; and the children in the congregation who had fidgeted during the earlier part of the proceedings were now lying back in a surfeited sort of coma. The last rays of the setting sun shone through the stained-glass windows, birds were twittering in the trees, the women's dresses crackled gently in the stillness. Peaceful. That's what I'm driving at. I felt peaceful. Everybody felt peaceful. And that is why the explosion, when it came, sounded like the end of all things.

I call it an explosion, because that was what it seemed like when it broke loose. One moment a dreamy hush was all over the place, broken only by old Heppenstall talking about our duty to our neighbours; and then, suddenly, a sort of piercing, shrieking squeal that got you right between the eyes and ran all the way down your spine and out at the soles of your feet.

'EE-ee-ee-ee-ee! Oo-ee! Ee-ee-ee-ee!'

It sounded like about six hundred pigs having their tails twisted simultaneously, but it was simply the kid Harold, who appeared to be having some species of fit. He was jumping up and down and slapping at the back of his neck. And about every other second he would take a deep breath and give out another of the squeals.

Well, I mean, you can't do that sort of thing in the middle of the sermon during evening service without exciting remark. The congregation came out of its trance with a jerk, and climbed on the pews to get a better view. Old Heppenstall stopped in the middle of a sentence and spun round. And a couple of vergers with great presence of mind bounded up the aisle like leopards, collected Harold, still squealing, and marched him out. They disappeared into the vestry, and I grabbed my hat and legged it round to the stage-door, full of apprehension and what not. I couldn't think what the deuce could have happened, but somewhere dimly behind the proceedings there seemed to me to lurk the hand of the blighter Steggles.

By the time I got there and managed to get someone to open the door, which was locked, the service seemed to be over. Old Heppenstall was standing in the middle of a crowd of choir-boys and vergers and sextons and what not, putting the wretched Harold through it with no little vim. I had come in at the tail-end of what must have been a fairly fruity oration.

'Wretched boy! How dare you – '

'I got a sensitive skin!'

'This is no time to talk about your skin – '

'Somebody put a beetle down my back!'

'Absurd!'

'I felt it wriggling – '

'Nonsense!'

'Sounds pretty thin, doesn't it?' said someone at my side.

It was Steggles dash him. Clad in a snowy surplice or cassock, or whatever they call it, and wearing an expression of grave concern, the blighter had the cold, cynical crust to look me in the eyeball without a blink.

'Did you put a beetle down his neck?' I cried.

'Me!' said Steggles. 'Me!'

Old Heppenstall was putting on the black cap.

'I do not credit a word of your story, wretched boy! I have warned you before, and now the time has come to act. You cease from this moment to be a member of my choir. Go, miserable child!'

Steggles plucked at my sleeve.

'In that case,' he said, 'those bets, you know – I'm afraid you lose your money, dear old boy. It's a pity you didn't put it on S.P. I always think S.P.'s the only safe way.'

I gave him one look. Not a bit of good, of course.

'And they talk about the Purity of the Turf!' I said. And I meant it to sting, by Jove!

Jeeves received the news bravely, but I think the man was a bit rattled beneath the surface.

'An ingenious young gentleman, Mr Steggles, sir.'

'A bally swindler, you mean.'

'Perhaps that would be a more exact description. However, these things will happen on the Turf, and it is useless to complain.'

'I wish I had your sunny disposition, Jeeves!'

Jeeves bowed.

'We now rely, then, it would seem, sir, almost entirely on Mrs. Penworthy. Should she justify Mr Little's encomiums and show real class in the Mothers' Sack Race, our gains will just balance our losses.'

'Yes; but that's not much consolation when you've been looking forward to a big win.'

'It is just possible that we may still find ourselves on the right side of the ledger after all, sir. Before Mr Little left, I persuaded him to invest a small sum for the syndicate of which you were kind enough to make me a member, sir, on the Girls' Egg and Spoon Race.'

'On Sarah Mills?'

'No, sir. On a long-priced outsider. Little Prudence Baxter, sir, the child of his lordship's head gardener. Her father assures me she has a very steady hand. She is accustomed to bring him his mug of beer from the cottage each afternoon, and he informs me she has never spilled a drop.'

Well, that sounded as though young Prudence's control was good. But how about speed? With seasoned performers like Sarah Mills entered, the thing practically amounted to a classic race, and in these big events you must have speed.

'I am aware that it is what is termed a long shot, sir. Still, I thought it judicious.'

'You backed her for a place, too, of course?'

'Yes, sir. Each way.'

'Well, I suppose it's all right. I've never known you make a bloomer yet.'

'Thank you very much, sir.'

I'm bound to say that, as a general rule, my idea of a large afternoon would be to keep as far away from a village school treat as possible. A sticky business. But with such grave issues toward, if you know what I mean, I sank my prejudices on this occasion and rolled up. I found the proceedings about as scaly as I had expected. It was a warm day, and the Hall grounds were a dense, practically liquid mass of peasantry. Kids seethed to and fro. One of them, a small girl of sorts, grabbed my hand and hung on to it as I clove my way through the jam to where the Mothers' Sack Race was to finish. We hadn't been introduced, but she seemed to think I would do as well as anyone else to talk to about the rag-doll she had won in the Lucky Dip, and she rather spread herself on the topic.

'I'm going to call it Gertrude,' she said. 'And I shall undress it every night and put it to bed, and wake it up in the morning and dress it, and put it to bed at night, and wake it up next morning and dress it – '

'I say, old thing,' I said, 'I don't want to hurry you and all that, but you couldn't condense it a bit, could you? I'm rather anxious to see the finish of this race. The Wooster fortunes are by way of hanging on it.'

'I'm going to run in a race soon,' she said, shelving

the doll for the nonce and descending to ordinary chit-chat.

'Yes?' I said. Distrait, if you know what I mean, and trying to peer through the chinks in the crowds. 'What race is that?'

'Egg 'n' Spoon.'

'No really? Are you Sarah Mills?'

'Na-ow!' Registering scorn. 'I'm Prudence Baxter.'

Naturally this put our relations on a different footing. I gazed at her with considerable interest. One of the stable. I must say she didn't look much of a flier. She was short and round. Bit out of condition, I thought.

'I say,' I said, 'that being so, you mustn't dash about in the hot sun and take the edge off yourself. You must conserve your energies, old friend. Sit down here in the shade.'

'Don't want to sit down.'

'Well, take it easy, anyhow.'

The kid flitted to another topic like a butterfly hovering from flower to flower.

'I'm a good girl,' she said.

'I bet you are. I hope you're a good egg-and-spoon racer, too.'

'Harold's a bad boy. Harold squealed in church and isn't allowed to come to the treat. I'm glad,' continued this ornament of her sex, wrinkling her nose virtuously, 'because he's a bad boy. He pulled my hair Friday. Harold isn't coming to the treat! Harold isn't coming to the treat! Harold isn't coming to the treat!' she chanted, making a regular song of it.

'Don't rub it in, my dear old gardener's daughter,' I pleaded. 'You don't know it, but you've hit on a rather painful subject.'

'Ah Wooster, my dear fellow! So you have made friends with this little lady?'

It was old Heppenstall, beaming pretty profusely. Life and soul of the party.

'I am delighted, my dear Wooster,' he went on, 'quite delighted at the way you young men are throwing yourselves into the spirit of this little festivity of ours.'

'Oh, yes?' I said.

'Oh, yes! Even Rupert Steggles. I must confess that my opinion of Rupert Steggles has materially altered for the better this afternoon.'

Mine hadn't. But I didn't say so.

'I have always considered Rupert Steggles, between ourselves, a rather self-centered youth, by no means the kind who would put himself out to further the enjoyment of his fellows. And yet twice within the last half-hour I have observed him escorting Mrs Penworthy, our worthy tobacconist's wife, to the refreshment-tent.'

I left him standing. I shook off the clutching hand of the Baxter kid and hared it rapidly to the spot where the Mothers' Sack Race was just finishing. I had a horrid presentiment that there had been more dirty work at the cross-roads. The first person I ran into was young Bingo. I grabbed him by the arm.

'Who won?'

'I don't know. I didn't notice.' There was bitterness in the chappie's voice. 'It wasn't Mrs Penworthy, dash her! Bertie, that hound Steggles is nothing more nor less than one of our leading snakes. I don't know how he heard about her, but he must have got on to it that she was dangerous. Do you know what he did? He lured that miserable woman into the refreshment-tent five minutes before the race, and brought her out so weighed down with cake and tea that she blew up in the first twenty yards. Just rolled over and lay there! Well, thank goodness, we still have Harold!'

I gasped at the poor chump.

'Harold! Haven't you heard?'

'Heard?' Bingo turned a delicate green. 'Heard what? I haven't heard anything. I only arrived five minutes ago. Came here straight from the station. What has happened? Tell me!'

I slipped him the information. He stared at me for a moment in a ghastly sort of way, then with a hollow groan tottered away and was lost in the crowd. A nasty knock, poor chap. I didn't blame him for being upset.

They were clearing the decks now for the Egg and Spoon Race, and I thought I might as well stay where I was and watch the finish. Not that I had much hope. Young Prudence was a good conversationalist, but she didn't seem to me to be the build for a winner.

As far as I could see through the mob, they got off to a good start. A short, red-haired child was making the running with a freckled blonde second, and Sarah Mills lying up an easy third. Our nominee was straggling along with the field, well behind the leaders. It was not hard even as early as this to spot the winner. There was a grace, a practised precision, in the way Sarah Mills held her spoon that told its own story. She was cutting out a good pace, but her egg didn't even wobble. A natural egg-and-spooner, if ever there was one.

Class will tell. Thirty yards from the tape, the red-haired kid tripped over her feet and shot her egg on to the turf. The freckled blonde fought gamely, but she had run herself out half-way down the straight, and Sarah Mills came past and home on a tight rein by several lengths, a popular winner. The blonde was second. A sniffing female in blue gingham beat a pie-faced kid in pink for the place-money, and Prudence Baxter, Jeeves's long shot, was either fifth or sixth, I couldn't see which.

And then I was carried along with the crowd to where old Heppenstall was going to present the prizes. I found myself standing next to the man Steggles.

'Hallo, old chap!' he said, very bright and cheery. 'You've had a bad day, I'm afraid.'

I looked at him with silent scorn. Lost on the blighter, of course.

'It's not been a good meeting for any of the big punters,' he went on. 'Poor old Bingo Little went down badly over that Egg and Spoon Race.'

I hadn't been meaning to chat with the fellow, but I was startled.

'How do you mean badly?' I said. 'We — he only had a small bet on.'

'I don't know what you call small. He had thirty quid each way on the Baxter kid.'

The landscape reeled before me.

'What!'

'Thirty quid at ten to one. I thought he must have heard something, but apparently not. The race went by the form-book all right.'

I was trying to do sums in my head. I was just in the middle of working out the syndicate's losses, when old Heppenstall's voice came sort of faintly to me out of the distance. He had been pretty fatherly and debonair when ladling out the prizes for the other events, but now he had suddenly grown all pained and grieved. He peered sorrowfully at the multitude.

'With regard to the Girls' Egg and Spoon Race, which has just concluded,' he said, 'I have a painful duty to perform. Circumstances have risen which it is impossible to ignore. It is not too much to say that I am stunned.'

He gave the populace about five seconds to wonder why he was stunned, then went on.

'Three years ago, as you are aware, I was compelled to expunge from the list of events at this annual festival the Fathers' Quarter-Mile, owing to reports coming to my ears of wagers taken and given on the result at the village inn and a strong suspicion that on at least one occasion the race had actually been sold by the speediest runner. That unfortunate occurrence shook my faith in human nature, I admit – but still there was one event at least which I confidently expected to remain untainted by the miasma of professionalism. I allude to the Girls' Egg and Spoon Race. It seems, alas, that I was too sanguine.'

He stopped again, and wrestled with his feelings.

'I will not weary you with the unpleasant details. I will merely say that before the race was run a stranger in our midst, the manservant of one of the guests at the Hall, I will not specify with more particularity – approached several of the competitors and presented each of them with five shillings on condition that they – er – finished. A belated sense of remorse has led him to confess to me what he did, but it is too late. The evil is accomplished, and retribution must take its course. It is no time for half-measures. I must be firm. I rule that Sarah Mills, Jane Parker, Bessie Clay, and Rosie Jukes, the first four to pass the winning-post, have forfeited their amateur status and are disqualified, and this handsome work-bag, presented by Lord Wickhammersley, goes, in consequence, to Prudence Baxter. Prudence, step forward!'

=13=
INDIAN SUMMER OF AN UNCLE

Ask anyone at the Drones, and they will tell you that
Bertram Wooster is a fellow whom it is dashed difficult
to deceive. Old Lynx-Eye is about what it amounts to.
I observe and deduce. I weigh the evidence and draw
my conclusions. And that is why Uncle George had not
been in my midst more than about two minutes before
I, so to speak, saw all. To my trained eye the thing
stuck out a mile.

And yet it seemed so dashed absurd. Consider the
facts, if you know what I mean.

I mean to say, for years, right back to the time when
I first went to school, this bulging relative had been one
of the recognized eyesores of London. He was fat then,
and day by day in every way has been getting fatter
ever since, till now tailors measure him just for the sake
of the exercise. He is what they call a prominent London
clubman – one of those birds in tight morning-coats
and grey toppers whom you see toddling along St
James's Street on fine afternoons, puffing a bit as they
make the grade. Slip a ferret into any good club between
Piccadilly and Pall Mall, and you would start half a
dozen Uncle Georges.

He spends his time lunching and dining at the Buffers
and, between meals, sucking down spots in the smoking-room and talking to anyone who will listen about

the lining of his stomach. About twice a year his liver lodges a formal protest and he goes off to Harrogate or Carlsbad to get planed down. Then back again and on with the programme. The last bloke in the world, in short, who you would think would ever fall a victim to the divine push. And yet, if you will believe me, that was absolutely the strength of it.

This old pestilence blew in on me one morning at about the hour of the after-breakfast cigarette.

'Oh, Bertie,' he said.

'Hullo?'

'You know those ties you've been wearing. Where did you get them?'

'Blucher's, in the Burlington Arcade.'

'Thanks.'

He walked across to the mirror and stood in front of it, gazing at himself in an earnest manner.

'Smut on your nose?' I asked courteously.

Then I suddenly perceived that he was wearing a sort of horrible simper, and I confess it chilled the blood to no little extent. Uncle George, with face in repose, is hard enough on the eye. Simpering, he goes right above the odds.

'Ha!' he said.

He heaved a long sigh, and turned away. Not too soon, for the mirror was on the point of cracking.

'I'm not so old,' he said, in a musing sort of voice.

'So old as what?'

'Properly considered, I'm in my prime. Besides, what a young and inexperienced girl needs is a man of weight and years to lean on. The sturdy oak, not the sapling.'

It was at this point that, as I said above, I saw all.

'Great Scott, Uncle George!' I said. 'You aren't thinking of getting married?'

'Who isn't?' he said.

'You aren't,' I said.

'Yes, I am. Why not?'

'Oh, well – '

'Marriage is an honourable state.'

'Oh, absolutely.'

'It might make you a better man, Bertie.'

'Who says so?'

'I say so. Marriage might turn you from a frivolous young scallywag into – er – a non-scallywag. Yes, confound you, I *am* thinking of getting married, and if Agatha comes sticking her oar in I'll – I'll – well, I shall know what to do about it.'

He exited on the big line, and I rang the bell for Jeeves. The situation seemed to me one that called for a cosy talk.

'Jeeves,' I said.

'Sir?'

'You know my Uncle George?'

'Yes, sir. His lordship has been familiar to me for some years.'

'I don't mean do you know my Uncle George. I mean do you know what my Uncle George is thinking of doing?'

'Contracting a matrimonial alliance, sir.'

'Good Lord! Did he tell you?'

'No, sir. Oddly enough, I chance to be acquainted with the other party in the matter.'

'The girl?'

'The young person, yes, sir. It was from her aunt, with whom she resides, that I received the information that his lordship was contemplating matrimony.'

'Who is she?'

'A Miss Platt, sir. Miss Rhoda Platt. Of Wistaria Lodge, Kitchener Road, East Dulwich.'

'Young?'

'Yes, sir.'

'The old fathead!'

'Yes, sir. The expression is one which I would, of course, not have ventured to employ myself, but I confess to thinking his lordship somewhat ill-advised. One must remember, however, that it is not unusual to find gentlemen of a certain age yielding to what might be described as a sentimental urge. They appear to experience what I may term a sort of Indian summer, a kind of temporarily renewed youth. The phenomenon is particularly noticeable, I am given to understand, in the United States of America among the wealthier inhabitants of the city of Pittsburgh. It is notorious, I am told, that sooner or later, unless restrained, they always endeavour to marry chorus-girls. Why this should be so, I am at a loss to say, but – '

I saw that this was going to take some time. I tuned out.

'From something in Uncle George's manner, Jeeves, as he referred to my Aunt Agatha's probable reception of the news, I gather that this Miss Platt is not of the *noblesse*.'

'No, sir. She is a waitress at his lordship's club.'

'My God! The proletariat!'

'The lower middle classes, sir.'

'Well, yes, by stretching it a bit, perhaps. Still, you know what I mean.'

'Yes, sir.'

'Rummy thing, Jeeves,' I said thoughtfully, 'this modern tendency to marry waitresses. If you remember, before he settled down, young Bingo Little was repeatedly trying to do it.'

'Yes, sir.'

'Odd!'

'Yes, sir.'

'Still, there it is, of course. The point to be considered now is, what will Aunt Agatha do about this? You know her, Jeeves. She is not like me. I'm broad-minded. If Uncle George wants to marry waitresses, let him, say I. I hold that the rank is but the penny stamp –'

'Guinea stamp, sir.'

'All right, guinea stamp. Though I don't believe there is such a thing. I shouldn't have thought they came higher than five bob. Well, as I was saying, I maintain that the rank is but the guinea stamp and a girl's a girl for all that.'

' "For *a*' that," sir. The poet Burns wrote in the North British dialect.'

'Well, "*a*' that," then, if you prefer it.'

'I have no preference in the matter, sir. It is simply that the poet Burns –'

'Never mind about the poet Burns.'

'No, sir.'

'Forget the poet Burns.'

'Very good, sir.'

'Expunge the poet Burns from your mind.'

'I will do so immediately, sir.'

'What we have to consider is not the poet Burns but the Aunt Agatha. She will kick, Jeeves.'

'Very probably, sir.'

'And, what's worse, she will lug me into the mess. There is only one thing to be done. Pack the toothbrush and let us escape while we may, leaving no address.'

'Very good, sir.'

At this moment the bell rang.

'Ha!' I said. 'Someone at the door.'

'Yes, sir.'

'Probably Uncle George back again. I'll answer it. You go and get ahead with the packing.'

'Very good, sir.'

I sauntered along the passage, whistling carelessly, and there on the mat was Aunt Agatha. Herself. Not a picture.

A nasty jar.

'Oh, hullo!' I said, it seeming but little good to tell her I was out of town and not expected back for some weeks.

'I wish to speak to you, Bertie,' said the Family Curse. 'I am greatly upset.'

She legged it into the sitting-room and volplaned into a chair. I followed, thinking wistfully of Jeeves packing in the bedroom. That suitcase would not be needed now. I knew what she must have come about.

'I've just seen Uncle George,' I said, giving her a lead.

'So have I,' said Aunt Agatha, shivering in a marked manner. 'He called on me while I was still in bed to inform me of his intention of marrying some impossible girl from South Norwood.'

'East Dulwich, the *cognoscente* informed me.'

'Well, East Dulwich, then. It is the same thing. But who told you?'

'Jeeves.'

'And how, pray, does Jeeves come to know all about it?'

'There are very few things in this world, Aunt Agatha,' I said gravely, 'that Jeeves doesn't know all about. He's met the girl.'

'Who is she?'

'One of the waitresses at the Buffers.'

I had expected this to register and it did. The relative let out a screech rather like the Cornish Express going through a junction.

'I take it from your manner, Aunt Agatha,' I said, 'that you want this thing stopped.'

'Of course it must be stopped.'

'Then there is but one policy to pursue. Let me ring for Jeeves and ask his advice.'

Aunt Agatha stiffened visibly. Very much the *grande dame* of the old *régime*.

'Are you seriously suggesting that we should discuss this intimate family matter with your man-servant?'

'Absolutely. Jeeves will find the way.'

'I have always known that you were an imbecile, Bertie,' said the flesh-and-blood, now down at about three degrees Fahrenheit, 'but I did suppose that you had some proper feeling, some pride, some respect for your position.'

'Well, you know what the poet Burns says.'

She squelched me with a glance.

'Obviously the only thing to do,' she said, 'is to offer this girl money.'

'Money?'

'Certainly. It will not be the first time your uncle has made such a course necessary.'

We sat for a bit, brooding. The family always sits brooding when the subject of Uncle George's early romance comes up. I was too young to be actually in on it at the time, but I've had the details frequently from many sources, including Uncle George. Let him get even the slightest bit pickled, and he will tell you the whole story, sometimes twice in an evening. It was a barmaid at the Criterion, just before he came into the title. Her name was Maudie and he loved her dearly, but the family would have none of it. They dug down into the sock and paid her off. Just one of those human-interest stories, if you know what I mean.

I wasn't so sold on this money-offering scheme.

'Well, just as you like, of course,' I said, 'but you're taking an awful chance. I mean, whenever people do it in novels and plays, they always get the dickens of a welt. The girl gets the sympathy of the audience every time. She just draws herself up and looks at them with clear, steady eyes, causing them to feel not a little cheesy. If I were you, I would sit tight and let Nature take its course.'

'I don't understand you.'

'Well, consider for a moment what Uncle George looks like. No Greta Garbo, believe me. I should simply let the girl go on looking at him. Take it from me, Aunt Agatha, I've studied human nature and I don't believe there's a female in the world who could see Uncle George fairly often in those waistcoats he wears without feeling that it was due to her better self to give him the gate. Besides, this girl sees him at meal-times, and Uncle George with his head down among the food-stuffs is a spectacle which – '

'If it is not troubling you too much, Bertie, I should be greatly obliged if you would stop drivelling.'

'Just as you say. All the same, I think you're going to find it dashed embarrassing, offering this girl money.'

'I am not proposing to do so. *You* will undertake the negotiations.'

'Me?'

'Certainly. I should think a hundred pounds would be ample. But I will give you a blank cheque, and you are at liberty to fill it in for a higher sum if it becomes necessary. The essential point is that, cost what it may, your uncle must be released from this entanglement.'

'So you're going to shove this off on me?'

'It is quite time you did something for the family.'

'And when she draws herself up and looks at me with clear, steady eyes, what do I do for an encore?'

'There is no need to discuss the matter any further. You can get down to East Dulwich in half an hour.

There is a frequent service of trains, I will remain here
to await your report.'

'But, listen!'

'Bertie, you will go and see this woman immediately.'

'Yes, but dash it!'

'Bertie!'

I threw in the towel.

'Oh, right ho, if you say so.'

'I do say so.'

'Oh, well, in that case, right ho.'

I don't know if you have ever tooled off to East Dulwich
to offer a strange female a hundred smackers to release
your Uncle George. In case you haven't, I may tell you
that there are plenty of things that are lots better fun.
I didn't feel any too good driving to the station. I didn't
feel any too good in the train. And I didn't feel any too
good as I walked to Kitchener Road. But the moment
when I felt least good was when I had actually pressed
the front-door bell and a rather grubby-looking maid
had let me in and shown me down a passage and into
a room with pink paper on the walls, a piano in the
corner and a lot of photographs on the mantelpiece.

Barring a dentist's waiting-room, which it rather
resembles, there isn't anything that quells the spirit
much more than one of these suburban parlours. They
are extremely apt to have stuffed birds in glass cases
standing about on small tables, and if there is one thing
which gives the man of sensibility that sinking feeling
it is the cold, accusing eye of a ptarmigan or whatever
it may be that has had its interior organs removed and
sawdust substituted.

There were three of these cases in the parlour of
Wistaria Lodge, so that, wherever you looked, you were
sure to connect. Two were singletons, the third a family

group, consisting of a father bullfinch, a mother bull-finch, and little Master Bullfinch, the last-named of whom wore an expression that was definitely that of a thug, and did more to damp my *joie de vivre* than all the rest of them put together.

I had moved to the window and was examining the aspidistra in order to avoid this creature's gaze, when I heard the door open and, turning, found myself confronted by something which, since it could hardly be the girl, I took to be the aunt.

'Oh, what ho,' I said. 'Good morning.'

The words came out rather roopily, for I was feeling a bit on the stunned side. I meant to say, the room being so small and this exhibit so large, I had got that sensation of wanting air. There are some people who don't seem to be intended to be seen close to, and this aunt was one of them. Billowy curves, if you know what I mean. I should think that in her day she must have been a very handsome girl, though even then on the substantial side. By the time she came into my life, she had taken on a good deal of excess weight. She looked, like a photograph of an opera singer of the 'eighties. Also the orange hair and the magenta dress.

However, she was a friendly soul. She seemed glad to see Bertram. She smiled broadly.

'So here you are at last!' she said.

I couldn't make anything of this.

'Eh?'

'But I don't think you had better see my niece just yet. She's just having a nap.'

'Oh, in that case – '

'Seems a pity to wake her, doesn't it?'

'Oh, absolutely,' I said, relieved.

'When you get the influenza, you don't sleep at night,

and then if you doze off in the morning – well, it seems a pity to wake someone, doesn't it?'

'Miss Platt has influenza?'

'That's what we think it is. But, of course, you'll be able to say. But we needn't waste time. Since you're here, you can be taking a look at my knee.'

'Your knee?'

I am all for knees at their proper time and, as you might say, in their proper place, but somehow this didn't seem the moment. However, she carried on according to plan.

'What do you think of that knee?' she asked, lifting the seven veils.

Well, of course, one has to be polite.

'Terrific!' I said.

'You wouldn't believe how it hurts me sometimes.'

'Really?'

'A sort of shooting pain. It just comes and goes. And I'll tell you a funny thing.'

'What's that?' I said, feeling I could do with a good laugh.

'Lately I've been having the same pain just here, at the end of the spine.'

'You don't mean it!'

'I do. Like red-hot needles. I wish you'd have a look at it.'

'At your spine?'

'Yes.'

I shook my head. Nobody is fonder of a bit of fun than myself, and I am all for Bohemian camaraderie and making a party go, and all that. But there is a line, and we Woosters know when to draw it.

'It can't be done,' I said austerely. 'Not spines. Knees, yes. Spines, no,' I said.

She seemed surprised.

'Well,' she said, 'you're a funny sort of doctor, I must say.'

I'm pretty quick, as I said before, and I began to see that something in the nature of a misunderstanding must have arisen.

'Doctor?'

'Well, you call yourself a doctor, don't you?'

'Did you think I was a doctor?'

'Aren't you a doctor?'

'No. Not a doctor.'

We had got it straightened out. The scales had fallen from our eyes. We knew where we were.

I had suspected that she was a genial soul. She now endorsed this view. I don't think I have ever heard a woman laugh so heartily.

'Well, that's the best thing!' she said, borrowing my handkerchief to wipe her eyes. 'Did you ever! But, if you aren't the doctor, who are you?'

'Wooster's the name. I came to see Miss Platt.'

'What about?'

This was the moment, of course, when I should have come out with the cheque and sprung the big effort. But somehow I couldn't make it. You know how it is. Offering people money to release your uncle is a scaly enough job at best, and when the atmosphere's not right the shot simply isn't on the board.

'Oh, just came to see her, you know.' I had rather a bright idea. 'My uncle heard she was seedy, don't you know, and asked me to look in and make enquiries,' I said.

'Your uncle?'

'Lord Yaxley.'

'Oh! So you are Lord Yaxley's nephew?'

'That's right. I suppose he's always popping in and out here what?'

214

'No. I've never met him.'

'You haven't?'

'No. Rhoda talks a lot about him, of course, but for some reason she's never so much as asked him to look in for a cup of tea.'

I began to see that this Rhoda knew her business. If I'd been a girl with someone wanting to marry me and knew that there was an exhibit like this aunt hanging around the home, I, too, should have thought twice about inviting him to call until the ceremony was over and he had actually signed on the dotted line. I mean to say, a thoroughly good soul – heart of gold beyond a doubt – but not the sort of thing you wanted to spring on Romeo before the time was ripe.

'I suppose you were all very surprised when you heard about it?' she said.

'Surprised is right.'

'Of course, nothing is definitely settled yet.'

'You don't mean that? I thought – '

'Oh, no. She's thinking it over.'

'I see.'

'Of course, she feels it's a great compliment. But then sometimes she wonders if he isn't too old.'

'My Aunt Agatha has rather the same idea.'

'Of course, a title *is* a title.'

'Yes, there's that. What do you think about it yourself?'

'Oh, it doesn't matter what I think. There's no doing anything with girls these days, is there?'

'Not much.'

'What I often say is, I wonder what girls are coming to. Still, there it is.'

'Absolutely.'

There didn't seem much reason why the conversation shouldn't go on for ever. She had the air of a woman

who had settled down for the day. But at this point the
maid came in and said the doctor had arrived.

I got up.

'I'll be tooling off, then.'

'If you must.'

'I think I'd better.'

'Well, pip pip.'

'Toodle-oo,' I said, and out into the fresh air.

Knowing what was waiting for me at home, I would
have preferred to have gone to the club and spent the
rest of the day there. But the thing had to be faced.

'Well?' said Aunt Agatha, as I trickled into the sitting-
room.

'Well, yes and no,' I replied.

'What do you mean? Did she refuse the money?'

'Not exactly.'

'She accepted it?'

'Well, there again, not precisely.'

I explained what had happened. I wasn't expecting
her to be any too frightfully pleased, and it's as well
that I wasn't, because she wasn't. In fact, as the story
unfolded, her comments became fruitier and fruitier,
and when I had finished she uttered an exclamation
that nearly broke a window. It sounded something like
"Gor!" as if she had started to say "Gorblimey!" and
had remembered her ancient lineage just in time.

'I'm sorry,' I said. 'And can a man say more? I lost
my nerve. The old *morale* suddenly turned blue on
me. It's the sort of thing that might have happened to
anyone.'

'I never heard of anything so spineless in my life.'

I shivered, like a warrior whose old wound hurts him.

'I'd be most awfully obliged, Aunt Agatha,' I said, 'if

216

you would not use that word spine. It awakens
memories.'

The door opened. Jeeves appeared.

'Sir?'

'Yes, Jeeves?'

'I thought you called, sir.'

'No, Jeeves.'

'Very good, sir.'

There are moments when, even under the eye of Aunt
Agatha, I can take the firm line. And now, seeing Jeeves
standing there with the light of intelligence simply fizz-
ing in every feature, I suddenly felt how perfectly foot-
ling it was to give this pre-eminent source of balm and
comfort the go-by simply because Aunt Agatha had
prejudices against discussing family affairs with the
staff. It might make her say "Gor!" again, but I decided
to do as we ought to have done right from the start –
put the case in his hands.

'Jeeves,' I said, 'this matter of Uncle George.'

'Yes, sir.'

'You know the circs?'

'Yes, sir.'

'You know what we want.'

'Yes, sir.'

'Then advise us. And make it snappy. Think on your
feet.'

I heard Aunt Agatha rumble like a volcano just before
it starts to set about the neighbours, but I did not wilt.
I had seen the sparkle in Jeeves's eye which indicated
that an idea was on the way.

'I understand that you have been visiting the young
person's home, sir?'

'Just got back.'

'Then you no doubt encountered the young person's
aunt?'

'Jeeves, I encountered nothing else but.'

'Then the suggestion which I am about to make will, I feel sure, appeal to you, sir. I would recommend that you confront his lordship with this woman. It has always been her intention to continue residing with her niece after the latter's marriage. Should he meet her, this reflection might give his lordship pause. As you are aware, sir, she is a kind-hearted woman, but definitely of the people.'

'Jeeves, you are right! Apart from anything else, that orange hair!'

'Exactly, sir.'

'Not to mention the magenta dress.'

'Precisely, sir.'

'I'll ask her to lunch to-morrow, to meet him. You see,' I said to Aunt Agatha, who was still fermenting in the background, 'a ripe suggestion first crack out of the box. Did I or did I not tell you – '

'That will do, Jeeves,' said Aunt Agatha.

'Very good, madam.'

For some minutes after he had gone, Aunt Agatha strayed from the point a bit, confining her remarks to what she thought of a Wooster who could lower the prestige of the clan by allowing menials to get above themselves. Then she returned to what you might call the main issue.

'Bertie,' she said, 'you will go and see this girl again to-morrow and this time you will do as I told you.'

'But, dash it! With this excellent alternative scheme, based firmly on the psychology of the individual – '

'That is quite enough, Bertie. You heard what I said. I am going. Good-bye.'

She buzzed off, little knowing of what stuff Bertram Wooster was made. The door had hardly closed before I was shouting for Jeeves.

'Jeeves,' I said, 'the recent aunt will have none of your excellent alternative schemes, but none the less I propose to go through with it unswervingly. I consider it a ball of fire. Can you get hold of this female and bring her here for lunch to-morrow?'

'Yes, sir.'

'Good. Meanwhile, I will be 'phoning Uncle George. We will do Aunt Agatha good despite herself. What is it the poet says, Jeeves?'

'The poet Burns, sir?'

'Not the poet Burns. Some other poet. About doing good by stealth.'

' "These little acts of unremembered kindness," sir?'

'That's it in a nutshell, Jeeves.'

I suppose doing good by stealth ought to give one a glow, but I can't say I found myself exactly looking forward to the binge in prospect. Uncle George by himself is a mouldy enough luncheon companion, being extremely apt to collar the conversation and confine it to a description of his symptoms, he being one of those birds who can never be brought to believe that the general public isn't agog to hear all about the lining of his stomach. Add the aunt, and you have a little gathering which might well dismay the stoutest. The moment I woke, I felt conscious of some impending doom, and the cloud, if you know what I mean, grew darker all the morning. By the time Jeeves came in with the cocktails, I was feeling pretty low.

'For two pins, Jeeves,' I said, 'I would turn the whole thing up and leg it to the Drones.'

'I can readily imagine that this will prove something of an ordeal, sir.'

'How did you get to know these people, Jeeves?'

'It was through a young fellow of my acquaintance,

sir, Colonel Mainwaring-Smith's personal gentleman's gentleman. He and the young person had an understanding at the time, and he desired me to accompany him to Wistaria Lodge and meet her.'

'They were engaged?'

'Not precisely engaged, sir. An understanding.'

'What did they quarrel about?'

'They did not quarrel, sir. When his lordship began to pay his addresses, the young person, naturally flattered, began to waver between love and ambition. But even now she has not formally rescinded the understanding.'

'Then, if your scheme works and Uncle George edges out, it will do your pal a bit of good?'

'Yes, sir. Smethurst – his name is Smethurst – would consider it a consummation devoutly to be wished.'

'Rather well put, that Jeeves. Your own?'

'No, sir. The Swan of Avon, sir.'

An unseen hand without tootled on the bell, and I braced myself to play the host. The binge was on.

'Mrs Wilberforce, sir,' announced Jeeves.

'And how I'm to keep a straight face with you standing behind and saying "Madam, can I tempt you with a potato?" is more than I know,' said the aunt, sailing in, looking larger and pinker and matier than ever. 'I know him, you know,' she said, jerking a thumb after Jeeves. 'He's been round and taken tea with us.'

'So he told me.'

She gave the sitting-room the once-over.

'You've got a nice place here,' she said. 'Though I like more pink about. It's so cheerful. What's that you've got there? Cocktails?'

'Martini with a spot of absinthe,' I said, beginning to pour.

She gave a girlish squeal.

'Don't you try to make me drink that stuff! Do you

know what would happen if I touched one of those things? I'd be racked with pain. What they do to the lining of your stomach!'

'Oh, I don't know.'

'I do. If you had been a barmaid as long as I was, you'd know, too.'

'Oh – er – were you a barmaid?'

'For years, when I was younger than I am. At the Criterion.'

I dropped the shaker.

'There!' she said, pointing the moral. 'That's through drinking that stuff. Makes your hand wobble. What I always used to say to the boys was, "Port, if you like. Port's wholesome. I appreciate a drop of port myself. But these new-fangled messes from America, no." But they would never listen to me.'

I was eyeing her warily. Of course, there must have been thousands of barmaids at the Criterion in its time, but still it gave one a bit of a start. It was years ago that Uncle George's dash at a *mésalliance* had occurred – long before he came into the title – but the Wooster clan still quivered at the name of the Criterion.

'Er – when you were at the Cri.,' I said, 'did you ever happen to run into a fellow of my name?'

'I've forgotten what it is. I'm always silly about names.'

'Wooster.'

'Wooster! When you were there yesterday I thought you said Foster. Wooster! Did I run into a fellow named Wooster? Well! Why, George Wooster and me – Piggy, I used to call him – were going off to the registrar's, only his family heard of it and interfered. They offered me a lot of money to give him up, and, like a silly girl, I let them persuade me. If I've wondered once what

221

became of him, I've wondered a thousand times. Is he a relation of yours?'

'Excuse me,' I said. 'I just want a word with Jeeves.' I legged it for the pantry.

'Jeeves!'

'Sir?'

'Do you know what's happened?'

'No, sir.'

'This female – '

'Sir?'

'She's Uncle George's barmaid!'

'Sir?'

'Oh, dash it, you must have heard of Uncle George's barmaid. You know all the family history. The barmaid he wanted to marry years ago.'

'Ah, yes, sir.'

'She's the only woman he ever loved. He's told me so a million times. Every time he gets to the fourth whisky-and-potash, he always becomes maudlin about this female. What a dashed bit of bad luck! The first thing we know, the call of the past will be echoing in his heart. I can feel it, Jeeves. She's just his sort. The first thing she did when she came in was to start talking about the lining of her stomach. You see the hideous significance of that, Jeeves? The lining of his stomach is Uncle George's favourite topic of conversation. It means that he and she are kindred souls. This woman and he will be like – '

'Deep calling to deep, sir?'

'Exactly.'

'Most disturbing, sir.'

'What's to be done?'

'I could not say, sir.'

'I'll tell you what I'm going to do – 'phone him and say the lunch is off.'

'Scarcely feasible, sir. I fancy that is his lordship at the door now.'

And so it was. Jeeves let him in, and I followed him as he navigated down the passage to the sitting-room. There was a stunned silence as he went in, and then a couple of the startled yelps you hear when old buddies get together after long separation.

'Piggy!'

'Maudie!'

'Well, I never!'

'Well, I'm dashed!'

'Did you ever!'

'Well, bless my soul!'

'Fancy you being Lord Yaxley!'

'Came into the title soon after we parted.'

'Just to think!'

'You could have knocked me down with a feather!'

I hung about in the offing, now on this leg, now on that. For all the notice they took of me, I might just have well been the late Bertram Wooster, disembodied.

'Maudie, you don't look a day older, dash it!'

'Nor do you, Piggy.'

'How have you been all these years?'

'Pretty well. The lining of my stomach isn't all it should be.'

'Good Gad! You don't say so? I have trouble with the lining of *my* stomach.'

'It's a sort of heavy feeling after meals.'

'*I* get a sort of heavy feeling after meals. What are you trying for it?'

'I've been taking Perkins' Digestine.'

'My dear girl, no use! No use at all. Tried it myself for years and got no relief. Now, if you really want something that is some good – '

I slid away. The last I saw of them, Uncle George was down beside her on the Chesterfield, buzzing hard.

'Jeeves,' I said, tottering into the pantry.

'Sir?'

'There will only be two for lunch. Count me out. If they notice I'm not there, tell them I was called away by an urgent 'phone message. The situation has got beyond Bertram, Jeeves. You will find me at the Drones.'

'Very good, sir.'

It was latish in the evening when one of the waiters came to me as I played a distrait game of snooker pool and informed me that Aunt Agatha was on the 'phone.

'Bertie!'

'Hullo?'

I was amazed to note that her voice was that of an aunt who feels that things are breaking right. It had the birdlike trill.

'Bertie, have you that cheque I gave you?'

'Yes.'

'Then tear it up. It will not be needed.'

'Eh?'

'I say it will not be needed. Your uncle has been speaking to me on the telephone. He is not going to marry that girl.'

'Not?'

'No. Apparently he has been thinking it over and sees how unsuitable it would have been. But what is astonishing is that he *is* going to be married!'

'He is?'

'Yes, to an old friend of his, a Mrs Wilberforce. A woman of a sensible age, he gave me to understand. I wonder which Wilberforces that would be. There are two main branches of the family – the Essex Wilberforces and the Cumberland Wilberforces. I believe there is also a cadet branch somewhere in Shropshire.'

'And one in East Dulwich.'

'What did you say?'

'Nothing,' I said. 'Nothing.'

I hung up. Then back to the old flat, feeling a trifle sandbagged.

'Well, Jeeves,' I said, and there was censure in the eyes. 'So I gather everything is nicely settled?'

'Yes, sir. His lordship formally announced the engagement between the sweet and cheese courses, sir.'

'He did, did he?'

'Yes, sir.'

I eyed the man sternly.

'You do not appear to be aware of it, Jeeves,' I said, in a cold, level voice, 'but this binge has depreciated your stock very considerably. I have always been accustomed to look upon you as a counsellor without equal. I have, so to speak, hung upon your lips. And now see what you have done. All this is the direct consequence of your scheme, based on the psychology of the individual. I should have thought, Jeeves, that, knowing the woman – meeting her socially, as you might say, over the afternoon cup of tea – you might have ascertained that she was Uncle George's barmaid.'

'I did, sir.'

'What!'

'I was aware of the fact, sir.'

'Then you must have known what would happen if she came to lunch and met him.'

'Yes, sir.'

'Well, I'm dashed!'

'If I might explain, sir. The young man Smethurst, who is greatly attached to the young person, is an intimate friend of mine. He applied to me some little while

back in the hope that I might be able to do something
to ensure that the young person followed the dictates
of her heart and refrained from permitting herself to be
lured by gold and the glamour of his lordship's position.
There will now be no obstacle to their union.'

'I see. "Little acts of unremembered kindness,"
what?'

'Precisely, sir.'

'And how about Uncle George? You've landed him
pretty nicely in the cart.'

'No, sir, if I may take the liberty of opposing your
view. I fancy that Mrs Wilberforce should make an
ideal mate for his lordship. If there was a defect in his
lordship's mode of life, it was that he was a little unduly
attached to the pleasures of the table – '

'Ate like a pig, you mean?'

'I would not have ventured to put it in quite that
way, sir, but the expression does meet the facts of the
case. He was also inclined to drink rather more than
his medical adviser would have approved of. Elderly
bachelors who are wealthy and without occupation tend
somewhat frequently to fall into this error, sir. The
future Lady Yaxley will check this. Indeed, I overheard
her ladyship saying as much as I brought in the fish.
She was commenting on a certain puffiness of the face
which had been absent in his lordship's appearance
in the earlier days of their acquaintanceship, and she
observed that his lordship needed looking after. I fancy,
sir, that you will find the union will turn out an
extremely satisfactory one.'

It was – what's the word I want? – it was plausible,
of course, but still I shook the onion.

'But, Jeeves!'

'Sir?'

226

'She *is*, as you remarked not long ago, definitely of the people.'

He looked at me in a reproachful sort of way.

'Sturdy lower-middle-class stock, sir.'

'H'm!'

'Sir?'

'I said "H'm!" Jeeves.'

'Besides, sir, remembering what the poet Tennyson said: "Kind hearts are more than coronets".'

'And which of us is going to tell Aunt Agatha that?'

'If I might make the suggestion, sir, I would advise that we omitted to communicate with Mrs Spenser Gregson in any way. I have your suitcase practically packed. It would be a matter of but a few minutes to bring the car round from the garage – '

'And off over the horizon to where men are men?'

'Precisely, sir.'

'Jeeves,' I said. 'I'm not sure that even now I can altogether see eye to eye with you regarding your recent activities. You think you have scattered light and sweetness on every side. I am not so sure. However, with this latest suggestion you have rung the bell. I examine it narrowly and I find no flaw in it. It is the goods. I'll get the car at once.'

'Very good, sir.'

'Remember what the poet Shakespeare said, Jeeves.'

'What was that, sir?'

' "Exit hurriedly, pursued by a bear." You'll find it in one of his plays. I remember drawing a picture of it on the side of the page, when I was at school.'

Bestselling Fiction

☐ No Enemy But Time	Evelyn Anthony	£2.95
☐ The Lilac Bus	Maeve Binchy	£2.99
☐ Prime Time	Joan Collins	£3.50
☐ A World Apart	Marie Joseph	£3.50
☐ Erin's Child	Sheelagh Kelly	£3.99
☐ Colours Aloft	Alexander Kent	£2.99
☐ Gondar	Nicholas Luard	£4.50
☐ The Ladies of Missalonghi	Colleen McCullough	£2.50
☐ Lily Golightly	Pamela Oldfield	£3.50
☐ Talking to Strange Men	Ruth Rendell	£2.99
☐ The Veiled One	Ruth Rendell	£3.50
☐ Sarum	Edward Rutherfurd	£4.99
☐ The Heart of the Country	Fay Weldon	£2.50

Prices and other details are liable to change

ARROW BOOKS, BOOKSERVICE BY POST, PO BOX 29, DOUGLAS, ISLE OF MAN, BRITISH ISLES

NAME..

ADDRESS ....

....

....

Please enclose a cheque or postal order made out to Arrow Books Ltd. for the amount due and allow the following for postage and packing.

U.K. CUSTOMERS: Please allow 22p per book to a maximum of £3.00.

B.F.P.O. & EIRE: Please allow 22p per book to a maximum of £3.00.

OVERSEAS CUSTOMERS: Please allow 22p per book.

Whilst every effort is made to keep prices low it is sometimes necessary to increase cover prices at short notice. Arrow Books reserve the right to show new retail prices on covers which may differ from those previously advertised in the text or elsewhere.

Bestselling General Fiction

☐ No Enemy But Time	Evelyn Anthony	£2.95
☐ Skydancer	Geoffrey Archer	£3.50
☐ The Sisters	Pat Booth	£3.50
☐ Captives of Time	Malcolm Bosse	£2.99
☐ Saudi	Laurie Devine	£2.95
☐ Duncton Wood	William Horwood	£4.50
☐ Aztec	Gary Jennings	£3.95
☐ A World Apart	Marie Joseph	£3.50
☐ The Ladies of Missalonghi	Colleen McCullough	£2.50
☐ Lily Golightly	Pamela Oldfield	£3.50
☐ Sarum	Edward Rutherfurd	£4.99
☐ Communion	Whitley Strieber	£3.99

Prices and other details are liable to change

ARROW BOOKS, BOOKSERVICE BY POST, PO BOX 29, DOUGLAS, ISLE OF MAN, BRITISH ISLES

NAME..

ADDRESS..

....

....

Please enclose a cheque or postal order made out to Arrow Books Ltd. for the amount due and allow the following for postage and packing.

U.K. CUSTOMERS: Please allow 22p per book to a maximum of £3.00.

B.F.P.O. & EIRE: Please allow 22p per book to a maximum of £3.00.

OVERSEAS CUSTOMERS: Please allow 22p per book.

Whilst every effort is made to keep prices low it is sometimes necessary to increase cover prices at short notice. Arrow Books reserve the right to show new retail prices on covers which may differ from those previously advertised in the text or elsewhere.

Bestselling Humour

☐	The Ascent of Rum Doodle	W E Bowman	£2.99
☐	Tim Brooke-Taylor's Golf Bag	Tim Brooke-Taylor	£3.99
☐	Shop! or A Store Is Born	Jasper Carrott	£2.99
☐	Cat Chat	Peter Fincham	£3.50
☐	Art of Coarse Drinking	Michael Green	£2.50
☐	Rambling On	Mike Harding	£2.50
☐	Sex Tips For Girls	Cynthia Heimel	£2.95
☐	Tales From Witney Scrotum	Peter Tinniswood	£2.50
☐	Tales From A Long Room	Peter Tinniswood	£2.75
☐	Uncle Mort's North Country	Peter Tinniswood	£2.50
☐	Five Hundred Mile Walkies	Mark Wallington	£2.50

Prices and other details are liable to change

ARROW BOOKS, BOOKSERVICE BY POST, PO BOX 29, DOUGLAS, ISLE
OF MAN, BRITISH ISLES

NAME...

ADDRESS..

....

....

Please enclose a cheque or postal order made out to Arrow Books Ltd. for the amount
due and allow the following for postage and packing.

U.K. CUSTOMERS: Please allow 22p per book to a maximum of £3.00.

B.F.P.O. & EIRE: Please allow 22p per book to a maximum of £3.00.

OVERSEAS CUSTOMERS: Please allow 22p per book.

Whilst every effort is made to keep prices low it is sometimes necessary to increase cover
prices at short notice. Arrow Books reserve the right to show new retail prices on covers
which may differ from those previously advertised in the text or elsewhere.